"Your eyes are the color of the sea," the gypsy said.

"Yet the sea has proved your enemy, not your friend. It has taken from you the two who were dearest to your heart."

Davinia gasped. This was incredible! For barely a year ago, her adored parents had been shipwrecked and drowned off the coast of Italy.

"The path of your life does not run smooth at present," the gypsy continued, her hands hovering around the crystal ball. "Ah! There is hope for you, my pretty one! I observe a tall, handsome man. He has dark hair and brilliant blue eyes. His name begins with the initial M."

"Are you quite sure?" ─────

The gypsy's bl───────────────────── ─── lies!" She looked su──────────────────, and she waved tow──────────────────. "Now go, my dear. Y──────────── ahead of you. But put your trus─────── of whom I tell you, and true happiness will be yours."

Novels by Caroline Courtney

Duchess in Disguise
A Wager For Love
Love Unmasked
Guardian of The Heart
Dangerous Engagement

Published by
WARNER BOOKS

ATTENTION: SCHOOLS AND CORPORATIONS

WARNER books are available at quantity discounts with bulk purchase for educational, business, or sales promotional use. For information, please write to: SPECIAL SALES DEPARTMENT, WARNER BOOKS, 75 ROCKEFELLER PLAZA, NEW YORK, N.Y. 10019

ARE THERE WARNER BOOKS
YOU WANT BUT CANNOT FIND IN YOUR LOCAL STORES?

You can get any WARNER BOOKS title in print. Simply send title and retail price, plus 50¢ per order and 20¢ per copy to cover mailing and handling costs for each book desired. New York State and California residents add applicable sales tax. Enclose check or money order only, no cash please, to: WARNER BOOKS, P.O. BOX 690, NEW YORK, N.Y. 10019

CAROLINE COURTNEY

Fortunes of Love

WARNER BOOKS

A Warner Communications Company

WARNER BOOKS EDITION

Copyright © 1980 by Arlington (Publishers) Books, Ltd.
All rights reserved.

ISBN: 0-446-94055-0

Cover design by Gene Light

Cover art by Walter Popp

Warner Books, Inc., 75 Rockefeller Plaza, New York, N.Y. 10019

A Warner Communications Company

Printed in the United States of America

First Printing: January, 1980

10 9 8 7 6 5 4 3 2 1

One

"Davinia, you must not! I absolutely forbid it!"

Impatiently, Davinia shook off her cousin's restraining hand. "Fiddlesticks, Charlotte! Where is your spirit of adventure? Surely you are curious to know what the future holds in store for you?"

Charlotte sniffed disdainfully. "I certainly have no desire to consort with common gypsies, cousin. And you know as well as I that Mama would strongly disapprove . . . Davinia! Come back here this instant! Come *back* I say!"

But the laughing Davinia was already running across the grass toward the gypsy's booth under the spreading oak tree. What was the point, she mused, her green eyes dancing, of coming to the St. George's Day Fair if one refused, like Charlotte, to enter into the spirit of the day?

The trees fringing the lush green expanse of

Kingsmead Fields were garlanded with gay red and white ribbons. The citizens of Bath were in merry mood today, sampling the hot meat pies and custard tarts, thronging round the hoop-la stall and skittles alley, and laughing at the contortions of the young lads bobbing for apples in a barrel. Bright-eyed children darted between the booths, the boys blowing toy bugles and the girls selling delicate posies of forget-me-nots and windflowers.

Spring is really here at last, rejoiced Davinia. She threw back her head, reveling in the warmth of the soft breeze as it ruffled her wheat-gold curls. Spring, glorious spring! Yet from Charlotte's frozen expression, as she stood stiff as a ramrod near the coffee stall, anyone would imagine that all of life was one continuous winter's day.

Charlotte had not wanted to come to the fair at all. But her father, Sir William Sinclair, had emphasized that as some of the servants were engaged in the St. George's Day pageant, it was only fitting that a representative of the family should be present to give them encouragement.

Lady Lydia, Charlotte's mother and Davinia's aunt, had proclaimed herself far too fatigued to attend:

"Fairs are such noisy happenings . . . all those shouting people . . . and the crush . . . I should be sure to develop one of my headaches. Charlotte and Davinia shall go. It may amuse them."

Charlotte had not been amused at all. Her brown eyes had closed in horror at the antics of the performing monkey. She had wrinkled her long, thin nose in distaste as the local farm lads clamored round the brew stall. And when one of the parrots escaped from its cage, and flapped round Charlotte's head, Davinia had feared that her cousin would dissolve into hysterics.

The two girls had been on the verge of making their way home to Chartcombe Court when Davinia spied the fortuneteller. Charlotte was outraged when her cousin suggested that they consult the gypsy. But her protests fell on deaf ears. The laughing Davinia had already reached the gypsy's gaily-colored booth.

"Come along in, my dear," murmured the dark-skinned woman. Her golden bangles jangled as she waved Davinia into a rickety chair.

Davinia slipped a silver coin into the woman's gnarled hand. On the table in front of her lay a crystal ball, gleaming like a mysterious pearl in the dim light of the booth. The gypsy waved her hands over it once, twice, three times.

Davinia held her breath, her lovely aquamarine eyes shining. What fun this was! Of course, she was too sensible to take a fortuneteller's predictions seriously. Nevertheless, it would be interesting to hear what the gypsy had to say.

"You are young, my dear," whispered the gypsy, staring intently into the crystal ball. "And your eyes are the color of the sea. Yet the sea has proved your enemy, not your friend. It has taken from you the two who were dearest to your heart."

Davinia gasped. This was incredible! For barely a year ago, her adored parents had been shipwrecked, and drowned off the coast of Italy.

The gypsy went on, "The path of your life does not run smooth at present. I see a jade-green aura around a brown-haired girl. She is jealous of you. She conspires against you."

Charlotte, sighed Davinia, thinking of her dis-

7

approving cousin. No doubt at this very moment Charlotte was preparing to rush home and tell Aunt Lydia about Davinia's scandalous exploits at the fair.

The gypsy's hands hovered round the crystal. "Ah! There is hope for you, my pretty one! I observe a tall, handsome man. He has dark hair and brilliant blue eyes . . ."

Davinia leaned forward, her face alight. "Is there . . . can you . . . does his name appear in the crystal?" she breathed.

"No, his identity is not revealed. Wait! The mist is clearing. I believe . . . yes, I can see the initial *M*. Indeed, it is quite distinct. This gentleman with an *M* beginning his name is the one with whom your destiny is linked."

"Are you quite sure?" whispered Davinia.

The gypsy's blue eyes flashed. "The crystal never lies!" She looked suddenly tired. Her head drooped, and she waved toward the opening of the booth. "Now go, my dear. You have a stormy time ahead of you. But put your trust in the man of whom I tell you, and true happiness will be yours."

Davinia thanked her and stepped out of the booth into the bright sunshine. She rubbed her eyes, feeling a little shaken by the gypsy's uncanny insight into the happenings in her life. And how strange that the woman should predict that she would fall in love with a man whose name began with an *M!*

Davinia smiled. Well, she was ahead of the gypsy there. For had she not already met such a gentleman? Her heart lifted as she thought of Lord Randal Maunsell. He was tall, handsome and blue-eyed. And while his reddish-brown hair could not strictly be described as dark, Davinia supposed it was unreasonable to expect the crystal ball to be perfectly accurate on every count.

She had first been introduced to Lord Randal at her parents' house in London. She had been barely out of the schoolroom then, whilst he was a dashing young man just going up to Oxford.

Then, a few months ago, whilst she was sheltering from the rain in a shop doorway in Bath, she had encountered Lord Randal again. He had recognized her instantly, and for fifteen minutes they enjoyed the most amiable conversation.

Davinia found his teasing wit and amusing anecdotes most diverting. Never before had she felt so radiantly alive in the company of a gentleman. So much so, that she had willed the rain to continue all day. But soon the sun broke through again, and she was compelled to continue on her way up Milsom Street to meet Charlotte.

Before they parted, however, Davinia was delighted to learn that Lord Randal (who usually resided in London with his father, the Earl of Belwood) intended to spend the spring and summer months at the family's imposing house in Bath.

Since that fortunate chance meeting in the rain, Davinia had frequently encountered Lord Randal . . . at the Pump Room . . . after morning service at the Abbey . . . or on a morning promenade with Charlotte around Queen's Square. On each occasion her heart had missed a beat just at the sight of him. Even on the grayest day, in Lord Randal's company it was as if the sun was ever shining.

Yes, Davinia smiled, I must confess, I am more than a little in love with him!

"You have been an age, Davinia!" Charlotte's furious voice cut through Davinia's daydreams. "I shall tell Mama about this directly we arrive home.

9

How dare you leave me all alone whilst you run off to have your fortune told? I could have caught my death of cold. Out of the sun that wind is positively shrewish!"

"There was no need for you to stand and wait. You were quite at liberty to accompany me," said Davinia mildly.

Charlotte tossed her head. From the corner of her eye, an amused Davinia observed her cousin biting back the question she was longing to ask. At last, as they reached their waiting chaise, Charlotte's curiosity got the better of her.

"So, what pack of lies did the gypsy tell you?"

Davinia affected a rueful expression as they set off toward Chartcombe. "Oh, I must own that you were right, Charlotte. She was really infuriatingly vague . . . except for the intelligence that I have a stormy time ahead of me."

"That at least is true," retorted Charlotte with smug satisfaction. "Mama will not be at *all* pleased at what I have to reveal to her."

Lady Lydia's angular face was a picture of reproach. "I declare, it is *too* disappointing of you, Davinia."

The ladies had changed for dinner, and Lady Lydia was resting on the drawing room sofa. She raised a limp hand, and Davinia hurried across with an extra velvet cushion to place behind her aunt's back.

"We took you in, Niece," Lady Lydia went on mournfully, "in all good faith after your poor parents' tragic death. Though I must confess it is still beyond me to reason why you were left in such desperate financial straits."

"My father," Davinia explained patiently, for at

least the tenth time, "had heavy losses with his stocks and shares. He was ill advised—"

"He was certainly ill advised to marry your mother," sighed Lady Lydia, pushing back wispy fronds of dark hair from her brow. "I warned him of her extravagance, you know. I knew no good would come of it. But he would insist it was a love match."

"And so it was," flared Davinia, her green eyes stormy. "They were deeply in love. And Mama was never foolishly extravagant. It was simply that she was not blessed with a sound constitution. Papa was obliged to spend a fortune on doctors' bills, and the trip to Italy was purely for Mama's health. They hoped the sunshine would do her good, but instead . . . the sea claimed them."

I may have been left penniless, thought Davinia passionately, but at least I have the warm memories of a happy, loving childhood. We were never rich, but I was more than content. Not for the greatest wealth in the world would I exchange my upbringing for that of Charlotte's. Her every whim is indulged. She is cosseted and thoroughly spoiled. Yet with all her good fortune she is by nature sulky, spiteful and selfish.

Lady Lydia closed her eyes. Clearly, the demise of Davinia's parents was too exhausting to contemplate. Charlotte, seated on a footstool near the silk-draped windows, hurried her mother back to the point:

"It is not as if the gypsy told Davinia anything interesting about her future, Mama," she tittered. "There was not so much a mention of a tall, dark, handsome stranger coming to sweep Davinia off her feet."

"Ah yes, as I was saying," Lady Lydia went on. "We are only too happy to have you here at

11

Chartcombe Court, Davinia. It is our sacred duty, after all. But I will not tolerate such unseemly behavior. Gypsies indeed! And with the servants there to witness your disgrace! It is not to happen again. Is that quite understood?"

"Yes, Aunt," murmured Davinia demurely.

She took up her embroidery, reflecting defiantly that it had been worth incurring her aunt's displeasure for what she had learnt from the gypsy. Was it not heartwarming to have it confirmed that her destiny was to be linked with the dashing young Lord Randal Maunsell?

She could well imagine the reaction of her aunt and Charlotte if they could read her thoughts. On the one side, there was nothing Lady Lydia would like more than to see her penniless niece married, and off her hands. But there was a major stumbling block to any prospect of marriage for Davinia.

That stumbling block was sitting by the window, idly sorting through a boxful of shells.

Charlotte was four years older than Davinia. It was, therefore, quite out of the question for Davinia to marry first. And even worse, for Davinia, the charity cousin, to marry a man who was heir to an earldom!

Not, Davinia told herself severely, that Lord Randal had in any way indicated that he desired to marry her. They had merely met, quite frequently, and passed the time of day together, each clearly delighted to be in the presence of the other. And yet Davinia was sure, from the look in his blue eyes, and the intimate note in his voice, that Lord Randal was more than happy to be in her company.

Davinia rethreaded her needle. If only Charlotte could find herself a husband! But this was a long-standing problem, one which had been occupying the Sinclair family since the day Charlotte came out.

Davinia studied her cousin as she sorted her shells into different sizes, ready to stick onto her shell picture of a fashionable lady in her garden. It had to be admitted that Charlotte was no beauty. Yet she was by no means ugly. On the credit side, she was gracefully tall, and blessed with the celebrated Sinclair flawless complexion.

But on the debit side, her nose was a little too long, whilst her lank brown hair stubbornly refused to curl. And above all it was her expression, Davinia decided, which gave her such an unattractive air. Charlotte was forever frowning or glaring. Her constant complaining and pettishness lent her face a pinched appearance. If only she would laugh more, and learn to enjoy life, she would look quite a different girl, Davinia reflected.

"When you have quite finished staring at me, Davinia, perhaps you would rouse yourself to fetch my shawl from the morning room," said Charlotte. "I fear I may have caught a chill when I was waiting for you in that cold wind this afternoon."

With good grace, Davinia went to find the shawl. From her first hours at Chartcombe Court it had been subtly impressed upon her that in return for her board and lodging, she was to repay the family by fetching and carrying for Charlotte and her aunt. Inwardly, Davinia chafed and fumed at her situation. But there was nothing she could do about it.

Indeed, she reflected philosophically, if Sir William and Lady Lydia had not taken me in, what would have become of me? I should have been condemned to a dreary existence as a companion or governess.

She returned to the drawing room to discover Lady Lydia and Charlotte deep in conversation about Charlotte's twenty-fourth birthday, in May.

"Sir William and I have decided to celebrate the occasion by holding a ball for you, here at Chartcombe Court," said Lady Lydia.

"How lovely, Charlotte!" exclaimed Davinia, her eyes alight. "A birthday ball!"

Lady Lydia said carefully, "I think, perhaps, we shall not call it a *birthday* ball. After all, we do not desire to draw too much attention to your age, my dear."

"But twenty-four is not old!" laughed Davinia.

"It is when you are not married," pouted Charlotte, "and when everyone in the county knows you have never received so much as one proposal!"

"Do not fret," soothed Lady Lydia. "I shall ensure that some eligible young men are invited. I hear that Lord Alston has taken a house in Bath. If you remember, Charlotte, you were introduced to him during your London Season."

Charlotte cast her mind back through the years to the heady whirl of her London Season. Yes, she recalled Lord Alston. At the time, confident that she would be swept off her feet by a score of dashing young men, Charlotte had dismissed Lord Alston as dull, overweight and, being fifteen years her elder, far too old.

She wrinkled her nose. "But Mama, Lord Alston is already married, to that insipid Lady Penelope."

Lady Lydia shook her head. "The Lady Penelope took to her bed with a fever last summer, and sadly passed away. Lord Alston is left with three young children and I have it on good authority that he is searching for a new wife."

Davinia repressed a smile as she observed her cousin calculating the pros and cons of a match with Lord Alston. If she was honest, Charlotte would react with horror at the notion of marrying the portly Lord Alston, and assuming responsibility for his three precocious brats.

But Charlotte was too desperate to be married to indulge in the luxury of honesty. Davinia could almost hear her persuading herself that, indeed, there were many favorable aspects to be considered in marriage with a more mature man. A person of substance, who had left the follies of youth behind him . . . who would be enchanted with his new young wife and who would accommodate her every fancy.

And really, what could be more delightful than being presented with a ready-made family? The children would no doubt find their stepmother quite fascinating. She would quickly become their friend and confidante. More important, as Lord Alston was so comfortably situated, there would be a fleet of nannies and governesses to ensure that Charlotte need see the children for no more than a maximum of an hour a day.

"Yes," declared Charlotte brightly, "we must definitely send an invitation to Lord Alston."

"Davinia, would you be so good as to make a list of all the people we are inviting to the ball," smiled Lady Lydia. "I would do it myself, but my poor wrist fair aches from writing letters this afternoon."

Davinia willingly crossed to the pretty rosewood writing table in the corner of the drawing room. Taking a sheet of paper, she wrote in her clear, elegant hand, *Chartcombe Court Spring Ball*.

15

Underneath, at the top of the list, she inscribed Lord Alston's name. Then she looked at her aunt expectantly.

"I suppose we must invite Lady Selina Delvigne and her daughter," murmured Lady Lydia.

"Oh no, Mama!" exclaimed Charlotte. "I cannot abide the sight of Imogen Delvigne. She is quite odious!"

Lady Imogen Delvigne, as Charlotte well knew, was a plumply pretty girl with a fortune of 20,000 pounds to bring to her future husband.

"It will look discourteous if we cut them from our list," protested Lady Lydia. "Lady Selina always invites us to her dances."

Davinia kindly came to her cousin's rescue. "When I was conversing with Lord Randal after morning service last Sunday, he mentioned that Lady Imogen is very much in love with a major in the hussars. An announcement is expected when the major returns from his regiment at the end of the summer."

Charlotte beamed. "You are right, Mama. We must certainly invite her to the ball."

"And Lord Randal Maunsell too, of course," said Lady Lydia. "Until Davinia mentioned his name I had quite forgotten that he is currently residing in Bath."

Charlotte's eyebrows rose. "Lord Randal . . . he is extremely handsome . . . and is he not the heir to the Earl of Belwood?"

"Quite true, my dear. But he is," Lady Lydia searched for the most tactful turn of phrase, "he has only just attained his majority, Charlotte. I doubt if he will seriously be thinking of marriage for many years yet."

"You mean he will consider me too old," sulked Charlotte.

"I mean that he himself is too young to take on the responsibilities of marriage," soothed Lady Lydia. "Why, even if he were to offer for you, Sir William and I would have to think very carefully about the suitability of such a match. No, I feel you should direct your charms toward Lord Alston. He is a far more admirable man."

Davinia was relieved that Lady Lydia could not observe her flushed countenance as she bent to write Lord Randal's name on the invitation list. She did not for one instant believe her aunt's assertion that Lord Randal was too immature to contemplate marriage. What was more pertinent was that Lady Lydia knew from past experience how young men of Lord Randal's ilk were never attracted to Charlotte for long.

During her London Season, Charlotte had been escorted by many beaus as handsome, rich and eligible as Lord Randal. Yet one by one they had drifted away from Charlotte, and married girls who were no prettier than she, but who possessed all the wit and vivacity Miss Sinclair so sadly lacked.

Lord Randal will be coming to the Spring Ball, thought Davinia joyously. Oh, what a delightful evening it promised to be! Davinia loved to dance. And now she had the prospect of being partnered by the one man in the world who made her heart beat faster every time she so much as lifted her eyes to his. With his excellent figure and graceful bearing she was convinced he would prove to be the most accomplished dancer. And with Charlotte occupied in charming Lord Alston, there could surely be no objection to Davinia's spending much of the evening

17

in the company of a gentleman whom Lady Lydia herself had decreed quite unsuitable for her daughter.

Impulsively, Davinia turned to her aunt and declared, "It will be the ball of the year, Aunt! I am so looking forward to it!"

Before Lady Lydia could reply, Charlotte burst forth, "Oh, but it would not be seemly for *you* to attend, Davinia! You are only just out of mourning for your poor parents."

Lady Lydia raised a languid hand to her brow. "I confess, I had quite overlooked that. How right you are, Charlotte. No, it would not be at all proper for Davinia to be seen *dancing* barely a year after losing her dear Mama and Papa."

"But, Aunt," Davinia protested, utterly dismayed, "You know I mean no disrespect to the memory of my beloved Mama and Papa. Yet I am convinced no one would think it amiss if I attended the ball. Why, you yourself encouraged me to visit the fair with Charlotte today."

"Yes, and just look what happened," sighed Lady Lydia. "I am informed that you disported yourself in a bold, thoroughly unladylike fashion, rushing off to have your fortune told by a common gypsy!"

"At the ball, I should be a model of decorum, Aunt. I promise you!"

"I fear it cannot be, Davinia. That is my final word."

Charlotte sat smirking with satisfaction. Davinia could cheerfully have seized her cousin's twenty-four-year-old neck and throttled her. She is afraid, Davinia fumed, that because I am younger, I shall outshine her at the ball. Because of her petty, need-

18

less jealousy, I am to be deprived of a few delightful hours in the company of the man I love!

And what irony! For the only man for whom I should have eyes at the ball is the one whom Lady Lydia has dismissed as a possible husband for Charlotte.

It was not, of course, simply Davinia's youth which had caused Charlotte to veto her presence at the ball. It did not occur to Davinia, but it was an unmistakable fact that when the two cousins were present together at any gathering, it was to Davinia that all eyes turned first. With her shimmering golden curls, her lustrous aquamarine eyes, her spirited expression and graceful figure she quite unconsciously presented a charmingly refreshing picture. Especially when compared with the simpering manners and over-refined behavior affected in public by Charlotte.

Davinia's chagrin over the ball was denied further expression by the entrance of Sir William Sinclair. He was a short, stocky, bespectacled man with a permanently abstracted air, which Davinia found endearing but which irritated Lady Lydia exceedingly.

"Ah, there you are, William," she sighed. "Are you aware that the dinner gong sounded over fifteen minutes ago?"

Sir William assisted his wife from the sofa. "I am so sorry to be late, my dear. I was absorbed in the most fascinating article about miniatures. Did you know that King George has a watch that fits into his signet ring?"

"I am aware that *you* own at least four time-pieces, William, yet you still contrive to be late for everything. Now may we please go into dinner. This is the third time this week we have been delayed. If it happens much more I am convinced Cook will give notice, and you know how fatiguing it is for me to be constantly hiring new staff."

Once seated at the oval dining table, Lady Lydia laid down her soup spoon and remarked, "You must take the first opportunity to visit your tailor, William. You will most certainly need a new evening coat for Charlotte's ball next month."

The prospect of being fitted for a new evening coat plainly did not please Sir William. He was most comfortable in his oldest clothes, pottering on his bowling green, or closeted in his library. However, his eyes twinkled as he regarded Charlotte and Davinia. "Ah yes, the ball. No doubt you two young things will be dancing well into the early hours of the morning?"

Charlotte smiled, and said sweetly, "I am greatly looking forward to it, Papa. But Davinia, of course, will not be attending. Mama decided it would not be seemly, as Davinia is barely out of mourning."

Sir William frowned. "Lydia, what nonsense is this?"

Flustered, Lady Lydia ran nervous hands through her hair. "I thought . . . I merely wanted to do the right thing, William. After all, the quality of Somerset will be present, and some of the London *ton* too. I did not want Davinia to give the wrong impression by showing disrespect to her parents' memory."

"Gammon!" exclaimed Sir William. "I am convinced Davinia's parents would have wanted her to dance and laugh and enjoy herself. Not sit upstairs all by herself whilst everyone else is making merry below. Would you like to come to the ball, Davinia?"

Davinia ignored Charlotte's blistering stare. "Yes, I would, Uncle. Very much."

"Then that's settled," he declared firmly.

Lady Lydia signaled for the servant to bring in the roast chicken. "Really, all this fuss. I am sure it is of no consequence whether Davinia is present or not. It will, after all, be dear Charlotte's special evening."

"I must have a new gown!" cried Charlotte.

Sir William shook his head indulgently. "My, I have never known any girl to have so many new dresses as you, Charlotte. Did you not have something rather grand made recently for Sir Richard Irwin's ball?"

"Everyone has seen that," said Charlotte dismissively. "Davinia may wear it to my dance, and I shall have the modiste fashion me a lovely new gown."

As she spoke, she shot Davinia a spiteful glance which said: very well, you may come to my ball, but you will have to appear in a dress which everyone knows is one of my castoffs!

But Davinia's heart was singing. What do I care what I wear to the ball? I shall be there, that is the main thing. And Lord Randal will be present too. We shall converse, and dance and laugh and be happy together. I ask for nothing more.

After dinner, Sir William retreated as usual to his library. With a glass of brandy at his elbow, he was soon transported back into the amazing world of precious miniatures.

Charlotte and her mother seated themselves

21

once more in the drawing room to drink tea and ponder further on the question of the invitation list for the ball. It was clearly going to be a long and tedious task. Charlotte was determined to refuse an invitation to any unattached female who was younger, prettier or in possession of a larger fortune than herself. Determined not to become embroiled, Davinia quickly excused herself to step outside for a breath of fresh air.

She closed the drawing room doors behind her with a sigh of relief. There were times, and this was one, when she felt she could not tolerate one moment longer the sound of Lady Lydia's fatigued sighs, or Charlotte's impatient whine.

Of course she was grateful to Lady Lydia for taking her in and giving her a home. Yet, *home* is just what it is not, mused Davinia as she wandered through the rose garden. With Sir William shut away in his library all day, and Lady Lydia voluntarily confined to her sofa, Chartcombe Court is a very dull place indeed. My idea of a home is a friendly place filled with laughter and animated discussions between people of lively minds and healthy curiosity.

That is what Davinia had known until a year ago. It came hard for her now to find herself entombed in the gloom of Chartcombe Court. However, Davinia possessed too cheerful a disposition to remain melancholy for long. It was more in her nature to concentrate on the good things in life.

Her spirits soon lifted as she reflected on the beauty of this twilight hour. The wind had dropped, and the leaves on the trees lay still in the hush of the evening.

With a sure and silent step, Davinia made her way along a mossy path that led through the shrubbery beyond Sir William's bowling green. Apart from Davinia, no one ever visited this part of Chartcombe Court, so she found part of the way quite hard going, as the shrubs were overgrown and badly in need of pruning. But Davinia had no intention of mentioning the matter to the head gardener, as the last thing she desired was any attention brought to her frequent presence here.

At last, she reached a rusty iron gate set into a high wall which was smothered with creeper. Davinia pushed open the gate, and once on the other side, flung her arms wide and took a deep breath. For this side of the wall, to Davinia, represented freedom and privacy.

In fact, to be strictly accurate, she was trespassing. The land on which she now stood was part of the vast estate belonging to the Duke of Strathavon. But the gouty old Duke preferred to live in London. He seemed not to care a fig that his magnificent Elizabethan manor house, Avonley Chantry, was badly in need of repair, with his valuable acres lying overgrown and untended.

Davinia made her way down to her favorite place, the apple orchard. In one particular tree she had discovered a tree house. No doubt it had been erected there by a friendly carpenter for the present Duke when he was a boy. Davinia had come to regard the tree house as her own special retreat. She often came here, climbing up to sit hidden in the branches, reading, drawing or daydreaming.

This evening, however, she was content simply to wander through the trees. In the distance, on the other side of the orchard, came the sound of a low mooing. That would be Buttercup, she smiled, the cow belonging to Ben Jarratt, the village blacksmith.

As the Avonley Chantry estate was untenanted,

Ben found it very convenient to graze Buttercup there. And he was not the only villager who made illegal use of the land. Dotted around the estate were goats, hens, even a few sheep, all belonging to local people taking advantage of the Duke's lax attitude toward his land.

The Duke employed a baliff, of course, but he was a rogue most frequently to be observed supping ale in the White Hart in Bath. Lord Randal had pointed him out to Davinia once, as they strolled through the Abbey churchyard. The baliff, red-faced, had come lurching out of the White Hart, missed his footing and gone sprawling face down onto the cobbles.

Davinia wondered how Lord Randal was occupying himself this fine April evening. She shut her mind to the unwelcome notion that he might be calling on any one of the attractive ladies who resided in Bath. Instead, as she breathed the sweet-scented spring air, she encouraged her thoughts to wander to the forthcoming ball.

Would he, perhaps, lead her out of the grand salon and into the rose garden . . . there to declare his love for her? Once again, she heard the gypsy declaring that her destiny was linked with one who bore the initial *M*. It must be Lord Randal Maunsell! She knew no other gentleman in the world with that initial.

Oh, she sighed, there are three whole weeks to pass before the ball. Twenty-one long days. How shall I bear the waiting!

Two

As it fell out, Davinia found her days fully occupied in the weeks leading up to the ball. Lady Lydia, overwhelmed by the complexity of the preparations, retired to her apartments and delegated all the arrangements to her niece.

Davinia accepted the responsibility cheerfully, although she had never before in her life been called upon to organize an event of this magnitude. But she was an intelligent girl and reasoned that it was surely only a matter of refusing to be fussed, and exercising some good old-fashioned common sense.

It was fortunate that before the invitation cards were written, she had the wit to consult her almanac. What she discovered sent her scurrying up to Lady Lydia's boudoir. She found the lady reclining on her daybed, draped in a mantel of lavender silk.

"I am sorry to disturb you, Aunt, but I believe

it will be necessary to change the date of the ball. You see, on the night you favor, there will be no moon. As your guests will be traveling across country from all sides of Somerset, I imagine they would find it more convenient if there is some light to guide them. If we bring the ball forward a week, then we shall benefit from the full moon."

And I, she thought, shall only have to wait fourteen days instead of twenty-one before Lord Randal leads me onto the dance floor!

Lady Lydia raised a hand to mask her yawn. "Do whatever you think fit, Davinia. I leave it all to you."

Davinia devoted an entire day to writing out the invitation cards. Charlotte had promised to help, but at the last moment elected to go into Bath to select the material for her ball gown.

With the invitations dispatched, Davinia consulted with Cook over the menu for the buffet supper, and with Jarvis, the steward at Chartcombe Court, about the number of extra staff required to be taken on for the ball.

Davinia found Jarvis a tower of strength. He had served with Sir William and Lady Lydia for twenty-five years and it was largely due to him that the household functioned so efficiently. Davinia was happy to take his advice about the most suitable orchestra to engage, how the grand salon should be decorated, and which of the smaller salons should be set aside as a ladies' dressing room.

"I would recommend the room on the right of the entrance hall, Miss Davinia. The salon on the east side is, admittedly, more commodious, but it is rather near the servants' wing. Past experience informs me that the ladies are likely to be disturbed by the chatter of all the extra staff we shall have to engage."

"Oh yes, Jarvis. I had not thought of that. Now I wonder what we should do about the color scheme for the decorations in the grand salon? I believe Miss Sinclair has chosen to wear white to the ball, but I wonder which shade Lady Lydia will favor?"

This was a crucial factor. At Lady Selina Delvigne's Christmas dance the ballroom had been hung (in somewhat vulgar taste in Lady Lydia's view) with widths of red, white and green silk. To everyone's amusement Lady Selina herself had made her entrance at the ball draped in a scarlet, white and emerald striped gown "looking for all the world like one of the wall hangings," laughed Lady Lydia. Indeed, the entire county had been convulsed over the affair.

Such a disaster must certainly be averted at the Sinclair ball. However, Davinia's heart sank at the notion of once more mounting the stairs to her aunt's boudoir.

Jarvis coughed discreetly. "It will not be necessary to disturb her ladyship, Miss Davinia. In all the years I have served Lady Lydia I have never known her to wear other than a shade of palest lilac or palest blue to a ball. Your suggestion, therefore, of a pink and silver decor for the grand salon seems most appropriate."

Davinia sighed with relief. "Jarvis, whatever would I do without you?"

Late one afternoon, as Davinia was dressing for dinner, Charlotte sauntered, without knocking, into her bedchamber.

"I brought you this old gown of mine," she said, carelessly throwing onto the bed a dress of ice-green silk. "No doubt it will do for you to wear at

27

the ball. I must confess, that color was a dreadful mistake. Green is such a difficult shade. It tends to reflect quite horribly on the skin. But as the ball is in my honor, no one will be looking at you, so it doesn't signify what dress you have on." With that, she flounced from the room.

Curiously, Davinia slipped the gown over her head. How deliciously cool and fine the silk was! She reveled in the exquisite sheen of the fabric, reflecting ruefully that it seemed an age since she had felt the touch of pure silk against her skin. Naturally, she would have preferred to have a new ball gown of her very own. But in her present penniless state that was clearly out of the question. And Charlotte had worn this dress only once, so apart from a small tear at the hem it was in pristine condition.

But as Davinia eased her arms into the sleeves and pulled the dress down, her smile faded. How foolish of her not to have realized! Charlotte was a good four inches taller than herself. The dress was far too long. Not just at the hem, which was a simple matter to rectify. But the waist (which fashion that year dictated should rise high beneath the bosom) hung limply around her midriff.

Davinia studied her reflection in the long glass. "Well," she informed herself at last, "you would be wise to make the best of the matter. For you most certainly have nothing else to wear to the ball!"

Straightaway, she fetched her workbasket and took out scissors and pins. Over the next few days she devoted all her spare time to skillful alterations of the dress, snipping and tucking with all the art at her command.

Eventually, her patience and hard work were rewarded. She tried on the gown once more, and this time her eyes lit up. Now the length was perfect, with the hem swaying delicately round her trim ankles. The waistline was cut fashionably high, revealing the graceful curves of her trim figure. The color, too, looked delightful on Davinia. Whereas the pale green shade had not flattered Charlotte's coloring at all, it complimented Davinia's aquamarine eyes and English-rose complexion beautifully.

All the dress needs as a finishing touch, she decided, is a length of dark green velvet ribbon tied round the waist. Charlotte had announced her intention of taking the chaise into Bath the following day for a final fitting of her gown, and Davinia took the opportunity to accompany her, to purchase her ribbon.

"I shall be at least an hour at the modiste," Charlotte informed Davinia as they descended from the chaise. "I have quite definite notions on the set of the lace at the neck of my dress. I shall be obliged to give the dressmaker most precise instructions on how it is to be styled. But no doubt you will be able to amuse yourself in my absence."

In truth, Davinia was only too glad to have some time to herself in Bath. What a delightful city it is, she mused, especially today, bathed in May sunshine.

But then, even on the gloomiest days, Bath still retained a distinctive radiance—an effect evoked by the lovely golden stone with which most of the houses were built. For Davinia, Bath was a city of almost matchless beauty, with its elegant terraces and graceful crescents, all set in a hollow of verdant hills.

Davinia strolled down Lansdown Hill and entered bustling Milsom Street. She took some time over her selection of the dark green velvet ribbon, but at last she was satisfied and left the haberdashers well pleased with her purchase.

"Goodness, you have been an age! I was beginning to fear I should have to stand here till nightfall while you fussed around with your ribbons!"

Davinia smiled at the dashing young man executing an immaculate courtly bow right in the middle of Milsom Street. "Lord Randal! I had no idea you were waiting for me."

"I saw you enter the shop," he explained, "and resolved to persuade you to walk with me for a while. But I declare I have been standing here so long I can do no more than hobble, exhausted, to a seat in Sydney Gardens."

"Fudge!" laughed Davinia. "Why, you look the very picture of health." And so he did, appearing extremely handsome today in a dark blue riding coat, gray breeches and highly burnished boots.

His brilliant blue eyes held hers. "And if I may make so bold, you yourself look quite enchanting."

"It is all an illusion," confessed Davinia as they walked slowly up to Queen's Square. "I must confess I feel fair worn to a shadow with all the preparations for the forthcoming ball."

"Lady Lydia, I take it, has fallen into a swoon on her bed, and will not arise until it is time to dress for the ball," surmised Lord Randal dryly.

Davinia nodded. "You are nearly correct. In fact, it would not be so bad if she really would confine herself to her apartments and leave all the arrangements to me. But she will interfere. The other day, for example, I engaged for the ball an excellent orchestra who play in the Assembly Rooms here in Bath. To my horror I came across my aunt closeted with Lady Selina, arranging for the lady's own private musicians to play at the ball."

"Capital!" exclaimed Lord Randal. "Can you imagine two sets of rival musicians dueling on the front lawn of Chartcombe Court for the privilege of striking up the first cotillion! It almost makes me wish I were attending."

"Have you not received your invitation?" queried Davinia anxiously. "I wrote it out myself."

Lord Randal pushed back a wayward strand of reddish-brown hair. "Dash it, how remiss of me. I should have sent my man round with a polite refusal. But, well, I have had so many other things on my mind."

"You mean," faltered Davinia, "you will not be coming to the ball?"

"Previous engagement, I'm afraid, Davinia. Well," he looked a trifle shamefaced, "no, to own the truth this cropped up only a few days ago. There's a new, very exclusive gaming house opened in London. On the night of your aunt's ball, the Duke of Strathavon is hosting a party at the club, and I'm invited. Can't turn a chance like that down. The stakes will be sky-high, and I've wanted to match myself against Strathavon for years."

Davinia struggled to repress the disapproving note in her voice. Why should she condemn gambling? It was an activity in which most young men engaged. It would be foolish to expect Lord Randal to be any different from his peers.

He grinned. "Now, pray, do not put on your frosty face at the mention of a simple game of chance."

"It is merely that one hears of such vast sums, fortunes even, being lost after one evening at the card table . . . or on a single throw of the dice."

31

"Only the foolhardy lose heavily. I intend to win," he informed her. "I have no desire to go the same way as my notorious uncle. Do you know, he lost so much on the horses that whenever he crossed Newmarket Heath he would order the carriage blinds to be lowered, because he could not bear to face the scene of his disaster."

Davinia laughed. When Lord Randal was in such a lighthearted, amusing mood she found him utterly irresistible. How he raised her spirits after the gloom and unfriendly atmosphere at Chartcombe Court.

Lord Randal seemed anxious to turn the conversation from gambling. "I am most distraught, Davinia, that you have not complimented me on my new boots."

"Indeed," she protested, "I had noted to myself how fine they are. Such supple leather. And what a fine polish you have on them."

"Ah, but you have not seen the best part," he said. Lifting his boot, he displayed to her its sole, which had almost as fine a sheen as the upper.

"It is quite the thing in London, Davinia. Beau Brummell set the mode, and now all we bucks have our valets shine the soles of our boots with polish and champagne. Quite dazzles the eye, eh?"

"Davinia, do you normally disport yourself in public with young men who seem intent on imitating herons?"

Charlotte was regarding the pair with a contemptuous expression on her face.

Lord Randal recovered swiftly and bowed. "My dear Miss Sinclair. How delightful to see you again."

Charlotte inclined her head. "Good morning, Lord Randal." Then turning her back to him she said to Davinia. "The chaise is waiting, cousin. *If* you and your friend have quite completed your acrobatics on the pavement."

Lord Randall semed not at all put out by Charlotte's rudeness. Darting round to face her, he declared, "I waylaid Miss Davinia with the express purpose of relaying my heartfelt regrets that I shall not be free to attend your ball. Unfortunately, I have a prior engagement in London."

"How *very* disappointing," smiled Charlotte.

"I shall, however, take the first opportunity of calling on yourself and Miss Davinia after the ball.'

"I hope you will find us at home," replied Charlotte loftily. "I must advise you, we have *many* engagements."

Lord Randal winked at Davinia and escorted the two ladies to the chaise. When they had left Lord Randal behind, Charlotte said viciously, "Really, I cannot abide that young man! He is so . . . full of himself!"

"It is merely youthful high spirits," murmured Davinia. For herself, she felt as soon as they left Lord Randal that a black cloud had settled over her.

Charlotte sighed. "Indeed, *I* prefer a gentleman with a more mature attitude to life. Tell me, has Lord Alston accepted for the ball?"

"Yes, he was one of the first to send a reply," Davinia assured her.

"Then it is sure to be a most successful evening," smiled Charlotte. "My dress is beautiful, Davinia! Oh, I am so looking forward to the ball!"

So was I, thought Davinia sadly, until I learned that Lord Randal would not be present. How I wish he would not go to London, to this gambling house. I am sure no good will come of it. I feel it in my bones!

By the afternoon of the ball, hysteria at Chart-combe Court was reaching its height. Sir William, vague as ever, had omitted to instruct his footman to collect the new evening coat from his tailor. The footman was dispatched posthaste into Bath by Lady Lydia who declared herself mortified at the notion of appearing at the ball beside a husband dressed in that old, shabby evening coat.

No sooner was the footman out of sight down the drive, than screams of fury were heard issuing from Charlotte's apartments. Lady Lydia raised her eyes to heaven.

"Charlotte is quite impossible when she decides to throw one of her tantrums," she murmured. "Davinia, you must deal with this. I am going to lie down. My poor head is beginning to *throb*."

A few moments later Davinia saw Charlotte's maid, Annie, hurrying in shawl and bonnet from the servants' entrance of the house. Observing that the girl looked extremely harrassed, Davinia stopped her and inquired what was distressing her.

"It's Miss Sinclair's hair," sighed Annie. "You know how difficult it is to curl, Miss Davinia. Well, we've had it tied up in rags all morning, but it's still not right. So Miss Sinclair says I must go into Bath and purchase some special curling lotion." Annie shook her head. "Had I known ten minutes earlier I could have gone in with Sir William's foot-man. As it is, I shall be obliged to walk to Bath and back."

This seemed to the practical Davinia to be a complete waste of Annie's time. Especially as she would shortly be required to help her mistress dress. "What special hair-curling lotion is this, Annie?" she enquired.

The girl shook her dark head. "I am not rightly sure. Miss Sinclair read about it in the *Lady's Magazine*. It is made from exotic essences and makes your hair curl."

"It sounds like bottled moonshine to me," laughed Davinia. "Take off your shawl and bonnet, Annie. I will give you something that will prove far more effective than those exotic essences."

She rang the bell for the kitchen maid, and quietly gave her some instructions. Half an hour later, Annie hurried up to Charlotte's bedchamber holding a small vial of amber-colored liquid.

"Have no fear, I promise you excellent results," smiled Davinia.

Later that afternoon, Annie came rushing into the grand salon where Davinia was consulting with Jarvis over the final arrangements for the ball.

"Oh, Miss Davinia, I can't begin to thank you. Miss Sinclair's hair is a mass of lovely curls! Whatever was that lotion you gave me?"

Davinia's eyes danced. "We'll just call it Davinia's Delight," she laughed, and steadfastly refused to say another word on the matter. She could well imagine Charlotte's outraged howl of fury if she knew her hair had been dressed with none other than cold, sweet tea! It was a ruse Davinia had learned from her highly inventive mother. Although she could not be sure, she suspected that it was the sugar which in fact encouraged the hair to curl.

Having solved Charlotte's most pressing problem, Davinia turned her attention to troubles of her own. The ballroom, decorated in pink and silver, looked utterly charming. Everything was in place, with chairs set out along the sides, and cushions placed in the window arbors. In the adjoining supper room servants were busy bringing in the delicious cold collations which would lie under heavy linen cloths until the guests arrived.

"But where is the orchestra?" Davinia demanded of Jarvis. "It is nearly half past five. Guests will be arriving in another hour's time and surely the musicians should be setting out their instruments by now?"

Jarvis was imperturbable. "Do not fret yourself, Miss Davinia. Musicians are by nature somewhat eccentric creatures. One always worries that they will not be here in time. Yet almost at the very last second they arrive, all herded together in one carriage. Chaos appears to reign, yet within minutes they are in their positions, ready to play."

"I only hope you are right," murmured Davinia doubtfully, hurrying away to dress for the ball.

"My dear niece, how enchanting you look," exclaimed Sir William, as Davinia descended the main stairway to the great hall of Chartcombe Court, where the Sinclair family was assembling, ready to receive their guests. Sir William took a pace back, the better to admire the pretty picture Davinia made on the stairs. The golden ringlets framing her lovely face complimented perfectly the elegant Grecian line of the pale green dress.

"With your eyes, you should wear that shade more often," Sir William advised her.

Davinia curtsyed her thanks. She observed with a small inner smile that Charlotte's thin mouth was twisted with dismay as she regarded her cousin's splendid appearance in what she had been pleased to regard as one of her cast-off dresses.

Lady Lydia, swathed in lilac silk, leaned forward and examined the emerald necklace adorning Davinia's white throat. "Exquisite," she murmured. "I had no idea you possessed any fine jewelry, Davinia."

"It was my mother's. I have never worn it before because I did not own a dress which would do it justice."

Charlotte's face was ashen with rage. Oh, why had she been so foolish as to give Davinia that green gown? Now here she was, the center of attraction. And this was supposed to be a ball in Charlotte's honor!

"It is my opinion," said Charlotte, "that the emeralds are a little too showy with that gown, Davinia. Why not fasten on my pearls instead, and I will wear your necklace. It would contrast well with my white dress."

Nothing in the world would have persuaded Davinia to part with her mother's emeralds, even for a single evening. But she had no wish to engage in a confrontation with Charlotte on the matter. She said tactfully, "But your pearls flatter your lovely clear skin, Charlotte. And see how they compliment all the delicate embroidery on your dress."

"Davinia is right," said Lady Lydia. "You look charming just as you are, Charlotte."

Any further discussion was prevented by the arrival of the first guests. Davinia, meanwhile, was thankful to hear the sound of musicians striking up in the great salon. Jarvis was right. They had arrived, but only just in time!

By eight o'clock, all the guests were assembled in the pink and silver salon, and the dancing was set to begin. Despite her disappointment that Lord Randal was not present, Davinia nevertheless felt a flurry of excitement. How delightful, to be here at the start of a ball, with the prospect of hours of dancing and merrymaking ahead!

Dancing was one of Davinia's passions. Her foot tapped in time to the music as she glanced round the salon, watching the gentlemen approaching the ladies of their choice for the all-important first two dances.

Sir William, she noted, had gallantly engaged Lady Selina, whose ample form was encased in terra-cotta-colored silk.

"She resembles a *vase*," murmured Lady Lydia to Sir Richard Irwin as she stood up with him for the cotillion.

"Miss Davinia. You appear lost in thought."

Davinia found the large and somewhat overweight form of Lord Alston looming over her. He was in his early forties, with slightly bulging blue eyes and a pleasant, if vacuous expression.

Davinia smiled politely. "I was merely indulging in a very feminine fancy, my lord, and appraising the gowns of all the ladies present." She noticed Charlotte casting a scorching glance in her direction, and said hastily, "Do you not agree that my cousin Charlotte looks quite delightful this evening?"

Lord Alston cast a brief glance at Charlotte. "Miss Sinclair? Yes, to be sure. But I must confess, it is your own appearance which quite captured my attention, Miss Davinia. Why, your eyes are sparkling as bright as the emeralds round your neck. Come, I insist on claiming you as my partner for the first two dances."

Davinia gazed at him in dismay. Oh, this was not right. It was not right at all! Why had he not asked Charlotte, who was standing so expectantly, so hopefully, nearby?

Davinia was only too well aware that the highest compliment a gentleman could pay a lady was to engage her for the first two dances. Everyone would be eyeing Lord Alston to observe whom he approached. It was well known that he was seeking a wife . . . and how tongues would wag if she allowed him to lead her onto the floor.

And how furious Charlotte would be! She would surely make Davinia's life quite, quite unbearable.

The silence was becoming embarrassing. "I . . . er . . . Lord Alston . . . " Davinia faltered.

"Surely you would not refuse me? Am I really such an ogre?" he smiled. "I assure you I will not disgrace you. I am a most accomplished dancer."

With a leaden heart, Davinia accepted that to placate Charlotte, she must surely refuse Lord Alston. But that would disbar her from dancing a single step for the rest of the evening. For etiquette dictated that if a lady declined to dance with any gentleman, then it was the height of bad manners to stand up with anyone else.

Yet, there was nothing else for it. At all costs Davinia knew she must leave Lord Alston free to approach Charlotte, who at that moment was glaring most significantly at her cousin.

"Lord Alston, you are really most kind, but—" Davinia bravely began.

"Come along now, Lord Alston," called Sir William as he led Lady Selina onto the floor. "Stop pussyfooting around there, and bring Davinia to make up the set."

He hustled Davinia and Lord Alston onto the floor, and before Davinia could draw breath to utter further protest, the cotillion was under way. To compound the calamity, Davinia noticed that in the opposite set, Charlotte had been engaged by Sir Freddie Seppington, a pigeon-toed confirmed bachelor of fifty, with grog blossoms on his face that testified to his addiction to strong wine.

Never had Davinia enjoyed a ball less. Lord Randal, the man she loved, was far away in a London gaming house. Whilst she, Davinia, was uncomfortably aware that all she had to look forward to was an extremely acrimonious scene with Cousin Charlotte.

The evening passed in a blur for Davinia. She forced herself to laugh, to smile, and make the correct responses to her partners. She danced a minuet with her uncle and the Dashing White Sergeant with Sir Richard Irwin. He was Master of the County Hunt and danced with all the *brio* of one in full pursuit of the fox.

To her dismay, Lord Alston claimed her for the supper dance, and talked all the while of his rebellious younger son who had just set fire to his summer house. Charlotte, in a monstrous sulk, addressed not one word to Davinia. But this was not, Davinia realized, a happy state of affairs that was likely to last forever.

The storm broke the following morning. Launching straight into the attack, Charlotte marched into the breakfast room and shook Davinia roughly by the shoulders. "You deceitful, horrid girl! I shall never ever forgive you! Never, never, *never!*"

Her outburst aroused even Sir William from his customary morning stupor. "Charlotte! Have you taken leave of your senses! Sit down this instant and behave yourself as a young lady should."

Charlotte flounced into her chair muttering that Davinia had certainly not behaved like a lady last night. "More like a bold, grasping hussy. Oh, I was ashamed to acknowledge you as my cousin!"

Lady Lydia reached for her smelling bottle. "Charlotte is upset," she languidly informed Sir William, "because Davinia somewhat monopolized the attention of Lord Alston last night."

"He engaged me for but one single dance," pouted Charlotte, "and then he talked all the time about the poor grain harvest on his estate last year."

Sir William removed his spectacles and rubbed his eyes. "I cannot imagine," he said mildly, "why you are making such an infernal fuss about Lord Alston. You have no prospects there, Charlotte. And neither has Davinia, for that matter."

"Whyever not, pray?" inquired Lady Lydia loftily. "His wife died last year. I should have thought Lord Alston was a most eligible prospect for Charlotte."

Sir William shook his head. "I heard from Sir Richard Irwin, oh, more than a month ago that Lord Alston is fixed to marry a rather fetching Yorkshire widow. She has a couple of children of her own, so I understand, and plenty of northern common sense. Lord Alston feels she will soon have his own wayward offspring toeing the line."

Lady Lydia's knuckles were white. "Really, William! Why did you not *inform* us that Lord Alston was engaged?"

Sir William looked surprised. "I suppose it just slipped my mind. I did not imagine the fact to be of any importance."

Charlotte burst into noisy sobs. "Mama, what is to become of me? I do so want to be married!"

41

"Now see what you have done!" Lady Lydia accused her husband. "You have upset your daughter."

Sir William blinked rapidly beneath his spectacles, utterly bewildered. Davinia reached across and touched his arm. "If you have finished your breakfast," she said quietly, "perhaps we should make a start on cataloging the books in your library. If you recall, you said you would like me to help you with the task."

He shot her a grateful glance. "Yes, let us begin immediately, Davinia."

Together, uncle and niece slipped from the room, leaving the wailing Charlotte to the ministrations of her mother.

In the library, Sir William fell into his favorite armchair with an audible sigh of relief. "My, what a to-do. I never dreamed . . . I had no idea . . . but your aunt is right, Davinia. Something must be done about a marriage for poor Charlotte."

I could not agree more, thought Davinia. For with Charlotte unwed, there is no prospect of my friendship with Lord Randal being allowed to blossom into romance.

But where, oh where, can I possibly find a suitable husband for Cousin Charlotte?

Three

"What the devil do you think you're playing at? Come down here this instant!"

Davinia was so startled she nearly fell out of the apple tree. After a tiring week working in Sir William's library, attempting to restore order to hundreds of dusty tomes, she had escaped for a quiet hour to her favorite retreat in the Avonley Chantry estate. Surrounded by clouds of pink and white apple blossoms, she had been sitting peacefully with her sketch folder, enjoying the tranquility of this lovely May afternoon.

At least, everything *had* been tranquil until this harsh, masculine voice had disturbed her. Cautiously, Davinia peered through the leafy branches. To her horror, she found herself staring into the hard blue eyes of a tall, dark-haired and extremely angry man. Hastily, Davinia withdrew further into her tree house. Perhaps he had not seen her! Could he possibly have been addressing someone else?

His next words shattered her hopes. "I am talking to you, whoever you are, up there in my apple tree! If you are not down here, standing before me, within thirty seconds, I shall come up and throw you down!"

His furious tone left Davinia in no doubt that he was perfectly in earnest. Somewhat ruffled, and highly aggrieved by what she considered to be his unnecessarily imperious attitude, Davinia scrambled down to a lower branch and nimbly jumped onto the grass.

He stood with arms akimbo, glaring down at her. He was, she judged, in his early thirties. His dark brown cutaway coat and fawn breeches proclaimed him to be a gentleman of quality, though not a London dandy. And the lean, rugged lines of his face were endowed with a ruthless quality by the pronounced scar marking the skin just above his right eyebrow.

"Are you aware that you are trespassing on my land?" he demanded. "What is your name?"

Davinia flushed with anger. How dare he address her in such a high-handed manner? It was on the tip of her tongue to respond with a haughty, crushing retort when she realized how she must look in his eyes. She was wearing a shabby, shrunken smock which she had slipped on for her dusty work in the library. Her hands, her hair and she was sure, her face, were as grubby as a kitchen maid's. In no respect did she present the appearance of the niece of the respected Sir William Sinclair.

On the other hand, she mused, thinking fast, this cowling gentleman in no respect resembled the gouty old Duke of Strathavon. Yet he had the bare-faced nerve to tower above her, sternly maintaining that she was trespassing on *his* land. As the estate on which they stood quite definitely belonged to the Duke of Strathavon, the stranger's assertion could not possibly be true.

Well, Davinia decided, if you can play games my black-haired impostor, then so can I. Accordingly, she dipped the tall man a curtsy and whispered, "My name is Flora, Sir. I am a poor milkmaid from the village."

"And why," he inquired icily, "were you sitting up in one of my apple trees instead of attending to your duties?"

Davinia brushed some apple blossoms from her golden hair. "I . . . er . . . my cap blew off, Sir. In the wind. I had just climbed up to the apple tree to fetch it, when you called me down."

He was regarding her through narrowed eyes. "I see. So your name is Flora. And you are a milk-maid?"

Davinia nodded, beginning to feel a little nervous at the menace in his voice.

Suddenly, he seized her wrist. "Well, my pretty little milkmaid, I have a task for you to perform."

Before Davinia could draw breath to protest, he had hustled her through the orchard to the adjoining meadow where Buttercup, the blacksmith's cow, was tethered as usual.

Grimly, the black-haired stranger indicated the three-legged stool, and the pail set ready near Buttercup. "That cow needs milking," he declared. "Kindly set to work."

Davinia's eyes widened in horror. Mrs. Jarratt, the smith's wife, normally came up in the afternoon

45

to milk Buttercup. But today, of all days, she was late. And now this dreadful man was insisting that she, Davinia, should milk the animal. Oh, what have I done, mourned Davinia. It is all my own fault. Why was I so foolish as to masquerade as Flora?

Strong hands gripped her shoulders and pushed her down onto the stool. "Come now, Flora. I am waiting. We are *all* waiting."

As the impostor spoke, he indicated three tabby kittens who had crept near to the milking pail, ready to lap up the splashes of warm milk. Buttercup turned her head, her large soft eyes regarding Davinia doubtfully. She mooed softly, as if fully sympathizing with the golden-haired girl's predicament.

Davinia knew she could not milk Buttercup. She could not even attempt it. In fact, she realized, there was only one solution.

She leaped swiftly to her feet, kicked the milking stool toward the astonished dark-haired man, and ran for her life back through the orchard. If only I can reach the Chartcombe Court gate, she calculated, her heart pounding as she sped through the grass, I shall be safe. Once I am hidden in Sir William's shrubbery on the other side of the wall, then this frightening man will never know who I am.

Davinia dodged and weaved in between the trees, uncomfortably aware that the stranger was in hot pursuit. With his long legs and athletic bearing he had a natural advantage over Davinia. But she at least was familiar with the orchard. Not only did she know her way, but being small and lithe, she could slither underneath all the overhanging branches.

At last the rusty gate was within sight. With a sob of relief, Davinia flung herself at it. As she wrenched it open, an iron hand seized her round the waist.

"Oh no you don't, you little minx!"

The stranger whirled her round to face him. His blue eyes were glittering dangerously.

Flushed and disheveled, Davinia cast a longing glance at the open gate. So near and yet so far from freedom! If she could perhaps distract his attention . . . just one second would be enough for her to dart through the gate and into the safety of the Chartcombe Court grounds.

"I warn you," the impostor informed her quietly, "if you make one false move, I shall put you over my knee and spank you!"

Davinia drew herself up to her full five feet two and said indignantly, "How dare you speak to me like that!"

His mocking laugh rang through the apple orchard. "Ah! Now that was hardly the respectful tone of Flora the milkmaid. Could it be, I wonder, that you are not named Flora? That you are not, indeed, a milkmaid at all?"

Davinia reddened. "How did you know?"

Gently, he took her wrists in his. "Your hands, my dear."

Davinia cursed herself for her stupidity. Of course. Even though they were filthy from her day of sorting through the library books, her hands still had a soft, well-cared-for appearance. There was no disputing that they proclaimed her to be the lady she was.

She lifted her head defiantly. "My name is Davinia Sinclair. I am the niece of Sir William Sinclair, who owns the adjoining estate."

He raised a laconic eyebrow. "I must own to

being quite unfamiliar with country ways, and local traditions. Tell me, is it a customary diversion of yours, Miss Sinclair, to trespass on private property, to slither up and down apple trees and to masquerade (somewhat dismally I might add) as the local milkmaid?"

Davinia's beautiful eyes flashed. "And I would inquire in return, Sir, if it is a customary pastime of *yours* to adopt the manner and title of someone you are not."

"I? I am the Duke of Strathavon."

"I declare, you are pulling the long bow," flared Davinia. "You are not sixty-five years old. You do not—judging by your agility in pursuing me—appear to suffer from gout. In short, Sir, you are no more the Duke of Strathavon than I am the Princess of Wales!"

The stranger threw back his head and laughed. "Indeed, Miss Sinclair, I fear news travels slowly to this part of the country. My uncle, the old Duke, departed this world two weeks ago and I inherited the title. However much the intelligence may pain you, I fear you will have to accept that I *am* the Duke of Strathavon and you *are* trespassing on my land."

"Oh . . . I . . . beg your pardon. I was quite unaware . . ." Davinia was completely nonplussed.

But it only took a moment for her fighting spirit to come flooding back. "I must protest, my lord Duke," she declared boldly, "at your unwarranted and unjustifiably arrogant attitude toward me. I was doing no harm sitting up in the apple tree."

The Duke exploded. "Miss Sinclair, ever since I arrived here two days ago I have been fighting an uphill battle against the disorder on my estate. The chaos is indescribable. There are chickens and goats and sheep running amok all around the house. The farms are in the most appalling state of repair. My baliff—my ex-baliff—spends all his time in an inebriated state in one of the Bath taverns. The villagers bring their cows to graze in my fields instead of using the common land—"

"It is just that it is nearer, more convenient for them to come to your estate," explained Davinia. "And the common land is quite unsafe—"

"Do not interrupt! I have just received the most terrifying estimate for the cost of refurbishing the manor house, thanks to my late uncle's laxity in allowing it to fall into such a bad state of repair. I came down to the orchard hoping to escape from all my troubles, and enjoy a little peace and quiet. But even that little haven had been commandeered by you! It is just the last straw. I am beginning to wonder if there is a single inch of this estate that I can actually call my own!"

Davinia bridled. "Really, there is no cause to be so unpleasant. I can assure you I have no wish to set foot on your precious land ever again!"

He held open the gate for her. "That is excellent. I am delighted to hear it. Your words are music to my ears. For if you do come here again, I warn you, I shall personally take a horsewhip to you!"

With her head held high, Davinia walked through into the sanctuary of the Chartcombe Court grounds. The iron gate clanged behind her and the Duke strode off, back through the overgrown orchard.

Davinia was trembling with rage. What a thoroughly objectionable, arrogant, bad-tempered man the new Duke was! Well, he need have no fear, Davinia decided. All the beauty and peace of

Avonley Chantry is utterly spoiled for me now. I have no desire to go there ever again. And no desire to set eyes on the Duke again, either!

Davinia walked back to the house where she washed, changed into a fresh white muslin dress, and tidied her hair. She was about to join Charlotte in the drawing room, when she heard her cousin peevishly complaining to Jarvis that the fire was smoking.

"I fear, Miss Sinclair," replied Jarvis, "that the chimney needs sweeping. Unfortunately, this is difficult to arrange as Lady Lydia likes a fire to be lit in here all day, right through to high summer."

"Mama is naturally concerned about my delicate state of health," Charlotte informed him. "But there must be something you can do about the smoke, Jarvis. It is making me cough."

"As a temporary measure, I will arrange for some salt to be thrown on, Miss Sinclair, to settle the soot."

Davinia reflected wryly that Charlotte's alleged physical frailty never seemed to manifest itself in her voice. Indeed, when Charlotte was throwing one of her frequent tantrums, her screams could be heard as far away as the bowling green.

Still feeling shaken and angry after her encounter with the Duke, Davinia felt she could not endure an afternoon with a bad-tempered Charlotte. Instead, she slipped from the house and set off for the village. She was disturbed that Mrs. Jarratt had not come as usual to milk Buttercup. This was such a rare occurrence that Davinia wondered if Mrs. Jarrat was unwell, and in need of help and comfort.

As she strolled through the leafy lanes, Davinia's spirits began to rise. For who could remain downhearted for long when the earth and sky abounded with the promise of new life.

Drifts of bluebells formed an enchanting blue mist under the trees. And all around were the birds. A friendly robin hopped across the road in front of Davinia. Shy little wrens fluttered through a gap in the hawthorn hedge. Whilst high above, in the clear blue sky, came the welcome song of a skylark, singing its heart out.

Davinia paused for a moment, uplifted by the joyous sound. All the birds are in pairs now, she realized, as she watched them chasing one another from tree to tree. One would be a very dull clod indeed not to be infected by all the romance in the air.

It was spring and, inevitably, thoughts of love were never far away. Davinia's thoughts, naturally, soon strayed to Lord Randal Maunsell. How dashing and handsome he was. How amusing, how gallant! She uttered a wistful sigh as she entered the village, wondering when she would see him again.

In the main street, she waved a greeting at Mr. Jarratt, hard at work at his forge, and made her way round the back to the adjoining cottage. Naturally observant, Davinia noticed that some house martins had made a nest under the neat thatch.

To her relief, she found Mrs. Jarratt, looking hale and hearty, sitting outside the kitchen door with her pretty young daughter, Rosie. They were playing with an enchanting and very frisky mongrel puppy.

Mrs. Jarratt bobbed a curtsy as Davinia approached. "How good to see you, Miss Davinia," she said, her round, kindly face wreathed in smiles.

Swiftly, Davinia explained the reason for her

visit, carefully omitting all mention of her unpleasant encounter with the new Duke of Strathavon. "It was just that I heard Buttercup mooing and thought you might be unwell and unable to milk her," explained Davinia, bending down to throw a stick for the puppy.

"Bless you," smiled Mrs. Jarratt, "to own the truth, I was late going up to do the milking because my husband brought home this new puppy. Rosie was so delighted with it, and I was so pleased watching the child's face light up, I clean forgot the time!"

Davinia could well understand Mrs. Jarratt's feelings. Rosie was an enchanting red-haired child with mischievous blue eyes and the most beguiling expression on her pert face. She was indeed thrilled with her new puppy and it was clear that the pair of them were going to be quite inseparable.

"What do you intend calling the dog?" she asked Rosie.

The child wrinkled her freckled nose and said shyly, "I don't know, Miss. Will you name him for me?"

"If you'd like me to," smiled Davinia. She thought for a moment and then said, "Why, with that distinctive white mark over his eye, there is only one name for the dog. Patch!"

Rosie clapped her hands and laughed. "Come along, Patch! We'll go for a walk. I'll take you down to the bakery."

Mrs. Jarratt kept a careful eye on her daughter and Patch until they reached the bakery. Then she relaxed, and said to Davinia, "I expect you know, Miss, there is a new young master up at Avonley Chantry."

Davinia replied cautiously, "Yes, I had heard, Mrs. Jarratt. In view of the change of ownership, I wonder if it would be wise for you to continue grazing Buttercup up there. After all, it is private land and the new Duke may not take kindly to the village folk making free with his estate."

She considered it prudent to avert any future trouble by encouraging Mrs. Jarratt to remove Buttercup from the Duke's land before he ordered her to do so.

But Mrs. Jarratt seemed quite unperturbed. "Bless you, Miss. I've already had permission from the new Duke himself to leave Buttercup up there. I met him just now when I went to do the milking. I was all of a dither, I don't mind telling you, when he came across and told me who he was. I said I'd take Buttercup away at once. Then he asked why I'd brought her to Avonley Chantry in the first place. I explained all about the stealing rogues you get on the common land, and he said he quite understood, and I could bring Buttercup there as often as I liked. Well, I thought, what a charming gentleman. I was quite overwhelmed, Miss Davinia!"

Davinia could hardly believe her ears. Were she and Mrs. Jarratt talking about the same person? The same Duke? Then it occurred to her that of course the Duke had been pleasant to Mrs. Jarratt in respect for her mature years. But as she, Davinia, was clearly young and, he imagined, easily frightened, he had shouted and waved the big stick at her in an attempt to impress her with his power and authority.

Well, she thought angrily as she returned to Chartcombe Court, you have not impressed or frightened me one jot, my lord Duke! And somehow, some way, I shall devise a scheme to get even with you for your arrogance toward me. Just see if I don't!

Sir William kept the Sinclair ladies waiting half an hour for their dinner that evening. When they were all finally seated at the dining table, Lady Lydia was beside herself with rage.

"Really, William, it is too bad of you. Jarvis has just informed me that Cook is most unhappy at the way her food is continually spoiled by your habit of keeping everyone waiting for meals. He says she is muttering about taking up employment elsewhere. Though for the life of me I cannot imagine which household she is thinking of taking herself off to, as I know of no one in the immediate vicinity who is seeking a new cook."

Sir William pushed his spectacles up from his nose. "Ah," he murmured, "no doubt she is tempted by the notion of serving at Avonley Chantry. I understand the new Duke is seeking staff and will be considerably enlarging the household. My, what excellent soup this is. Mushroom, is it not? The flavor is not at all impaired by the long wait. I declare, Lydia, Cook fusses far too much. She should understand that just as the preparation of food is an art, so is the consuming of it. The digestive juices must be thoroughly whetted—"

"William!" Lady Lydia's voice was faint with strain. "What is this you say? Am I to understand that there is a new Duke of Strathavon?"

"Why, yes, of course." Sir William sounded surprised. "The old Duke passed away some weeks ago, and his nephew has succeeded to the title. I was sure I had informed you of the news."

Lady Lydia pushed aside her plate. "No, you

had not informed me. Merciful heavens! To think that my own servants were aware of this development even before I was! Really, William, I sometimes have nightmares that the Prince of Wales himself will arrive and catch me with my hair in papers because *you* have forgotten to tell me he was coming!"

Charlotte was rapidly becoming impatient with her parents' wrangling. "The new Duke, Papa. What manner of man is he?"

Sir William shook his head. "I know very little about him, my dear. He is, I believe, in his early thirties and has lived abroad for much of his adult life. I understand, however, that he has a rather doubtful reputation as a rake, and a gambler."

"But he is not married?" Lady Lydia pressed.

"Decidedly not," said Sir William, tapping his empty plate meaningfully with his fork as a signal for Lady Lydia to ring the bell for the next course.

Lady Lydia ignored him. The eyes of all three ladies at the table were alight with speculation.

This is wonderful news! thought Davinia. The very answer to my prayers. Why should not the Duke marry Charlotte? They are both selfish, arrogant and quite objectionable. It is as if they were destined for one another! Oh, if only a match could be arranged, then I will be free to encourage the attentions of Lord Randal Maunsell. Yes, I must lend Charlotte all my support!

A frown had creased Lady Lydia's brow. "I do not greatly favor this report of the Duke's dissolute reputation. It hardly sounds as if he would make a good choice of husband for our treasured Charlotte. With her delicate health, she requires a husband who will make it his first duty to attend to her welfare."

Davinia said reassuringly, "But, Aunt, most gentlemen spread their wings a little when they are young and living abroad. I am sure now that the Duke has inherited the estate, and all its attendant responsibilities, he will prove to be the most steady, reliable character. And I should imagine he must possess an enormous fortune."

"It is estimated at more than fifty thousand a year," nodded Sir William. "Lydia, are we to have a meat course, or do you intend to make me sit here until it is time for the pudding?"

Startled out of her reverie, Lady Lydia hastily rang the bell, and the roast lamb with capers was brought in.

"Davinia is right," asserted Charlotte, "I should very much like to become acquainted with the Duke. Shall you call on him, Papa?"

"I had not quite made up my mind," said Sir William. "As you are aware, the old Duke and I had that violent quarrel over that hundred acres of mine he wanted to buy, and we had not spoken for over ten years."

"Why did you and the old Duke quarrel over the land, Uncle?" inquired Davinia.

"As you know," replied Sir William, "the border of our two estates runs in a straight line, except for that long finger of my land which cuts into the Avonley Chantry estate. The old Duke was always eager to buy that hundred acres from me as the River Avon meanders through it, with some excellent fishing. I am no fisherman myself, but the Dukes of Strathavon have always been masters at the sport. Well, I was perfectly agreeable to sell the land, but then Strathavon insisted on haggling like a fishwife over the price."

"The old Duke was notorious throughout Somerset for his meanness," commented Lady Lydia. "He'd wear holes in his boots before he'd pay out for a new pair."

"In the midst of all the financial negotiations," Sir William continued, "I invited Strathavon to dine with me at my club in Bath. As I strolled toward the entrance at the appointed time, I heard the most fearful uproar going on in the street. Strathavon had arrived in a sedan, and was in dispute with the chairman over the fare. After many angry words had been exchanged, the Duke—his face purple by this time—drew his sword on the fellow."

Davinia exclaimed, "But, Uncle! How rash. The chairmen are infamous for their violent tempers."

Sir William nodded. "This fellow was no exception, He lashed back at Strathavon with his chair pole. At which point, it began to rain very heavily. Quick as a flash, the chairman whipped off the top of the sedan. Strathavon had to sit there, imprisoned and wet to the skin, until he consented to pay up!"

Charlotte laughed. "And that was the last you saw of him, was it not, Papa?"

"It was indeed. The Duke caught a bad chill from the episode and was so totally put out he withdrew to his house in Park Lane and never set foot in Somerset again."

The mirth died in Charlotte's eyes. "I do hope the new Duke has not inherited any of his uncle's unpleasant and eccentric characteristics."

Davinia smiled sweetly at her cousin. "I am sure you will find him the most charming man, Charlotte."

"You must call on the Duke directly, William," Lady Lydia instructed her husband. "Tomorrow afternoon."

Sir William squirmed uncomfortably in his

chair. "I am really most unsure about the matter, Lydia. After all, the old Duke and I were on such bad terms . . . "

"Water under the bridge," declared Lady Lydia.

"You have always instructed me to let bygones be bygones," murmured Charlotte.

"Besides, Uncle, the Duke is your neighbor," Davinia thought she should add some practical weight to the argument. "It is surely unwise policy to have an unfriendly relationship with those who live closest to you."

"Very well," sighed Sir William. "I shall call on the Duke tomorrow. And then perhaps your curiosity will be satisfied."

As soon as Sir William returned the following afternoon, Charlotte ran into the hall and pulled him into the drawing room. "Come and sit here, on the sofa next to me, Papa. Did you have an enjoyable time? You have been gone nearly two hours. What is the Duke like? Did you see a great deal of the house? Is he an amiable man? Is he likely to call on us? When—"

"Charlotte, compose yourself," murmured Lady Lydia, shooing her daughter off the sofa and reclining on it with a sigh of exhaustion. "Now, William, I trust you found the Duke at home?"

Sir William nodded, smiling his thanks as Davinia thoughtfully brought him a footstool and his silver snuffbox. "He was indeed in residence, though it would be a mistake to employ the word 'home' at present. He received me most civilly, and apologized for the somewhat chaotic state of the house. The old Duke let it go completely, you know, and his nephew has called in an army of refurbishers to get the place in order."

58

Charlotte opened her mouth to make further urgent inquiries about the Duke, but a warning glare from her mother silenced her.

"And what did you discover, William, about the Duke's nature and his future plans? Does he intend to reside permanently at Avonley Chantry, with a wife at his side, or will he be off on his travels again?"

Sir William seemed preoccupied with his snuff. "Mmm, this is an excellent blend, Davinia."

"Thank you, Uncle. I mixed it myself."

"William!"

"Ah yes, what was that, Lydia? Well, I must confess it did not occur to me to quiz the Duke on his personal affairs. Since you ask, we talked for a long time about the chimneys at Avonley Chantry."

"Chimneys?" queried Lady Lydia faintly.

"Yes, they are of a most unusual design on the manor house. The Duke's theory is—"

Lady Lydia seemed almost ready to fall off the sofa with impatient fatigue. "William, *when* will the Duke be calling on us?"

"In the next couple of days, he said. I told him we would all quite understand if he was compelled to delay his call because of his involvement in overseeing the renovations."

Davinia could not repress a smile as Charlotte's face contorted with rage at the idea of a delay in meeting the Duke. Unfortunately, Charlotte observed the upward tilt to her cousin's mouth.

When her father had left the room, she remarked, "It will not be necessary for you to be present, Davinia, when the Duke comes to call. After all, it will be Mama and I whose acquaintance he will be eager to make."

Lady Lydia had closed her eyes and appeared to be dozing on the sofa. Charlotte shot her cousin a look of triumph.

Davinia bent to her embroidery. My, Charlotte, what a perfect pair you and the Duke will make, she thought. And you need have no fear, Cousin. It will be with the greatest of pleasure that I shall be absent when the Duke of Strathavon comes to call.

Four

"Mama!" Charlotte came rushing in from the garden. "There is a gentleman on horseback riding up the drive!"

Lady Lydia frowned. "Charlotte, how many times must I tell you that ladies *never* run. It is so unseemly. You must strive for a slow, measured pace at all times."

Charlotte hopped from foot to foot in an agony of impatience. "Yes, Mama. I will endeavor to remember. But I am convinced our visitor is the Duke of Strathavon! And here am I wearing this horrid plain gown." She thrust her basketful of cut roses into Davinia's arms. "Take these, Cousin, and go away and arrange them whilst the Duke is here. I must ring for Annie. She shall help me change into my new embroidered muslin."

Davinia had wandered to the window, the closer to observe their unexpected caller. "I fear you are mistaken, Charlotte. The gentleman on horseback is not the Duke of Strathavon, but Lord Randal Maunsell. If you recall, he promised to wait on us after the ball."

Charlotte's face fell. "I shall certainly not bother changing my dress for *him*. A dandy like Lord Randal reserves his admiring glances for his own attire, never mine."

"You will indeed make yourself presentable, Charlotte," instructed Lady Lydia with quiet authority. "Are you not aware that Lord Randal is a second cousin to the new Duke of Strathavon? It is important that you make the best possible impression on Lord Randal. You know how men gossip together at their clubs and over their after-dinner port. We must ensure that Lord Randal speaks of you in the most glowing terms to his cousin."

"Why, yes, of course," exclaimed Charlotte. "And if we are charming to Lord Randal, perhaps he will divulge to us more of the Duke's future plans." She rounded on Davinia. "Cousin, Lord Randal is always most agreeable toward you. I am relying on you to encourage him to tell us all he knows about the Duke of Strathavon."

Oh, how Davinia longed to set eyes on Lord Randal again! After the tension-filled atmosphere of Chartcombe Court, it was like a welcome breath of fresh air hearing Lord Randal's distinctive voice in the hall as Jarvis took his gloves and riding whip.

Within a few minutes, Lord Randal was seated in the drawing room with Lady Lydia solicitously offering him wine refreshment. He was as dashingly dressed as ever, in a dark green riding coat and emerald silk waistcoat.

Yet, to Davinia's observant and loving eye he looked a little less carefree than on their last meeting. His step on entering had not the jaunty spring she associated with him. His shoulders drooped slightly, and there were deep shadows of fatigue beneath his blue eyes.

Her heart went out to him. What could possibly be wrong? Although his conversation was as light and amusing as ever, she could sense that the handsome young man had weighty matters on his mind.

With Lord Randal's courteous, formal inquiries into the health and well-bring of the Sinclair family completed, Charlotte said, with a meaningful glance at Davinia:

"No doubt you have heard, my lord, that Avonley Chantry is to be reopened?"

Lord Randal nodded, rather gloomily. "That is correct. My cousin, the Duke of Strathavon, has set in motion extremely elaborate and costly plans for the restoration of the house."

"Surely," inquired Davinia, "he does not intend to live in such a vast establishment alone? Or perhaps he means to let the house, whilst he is away traveling in Europe?"

Charlotte and her mother gave their full attention to Lord Randal's reply:

"Oh, Strathavon's traveling days are over, so I hear. He tells me he's been everywhere he ever desired to go, and now he's content to reside in England. In any case, he'll be too occupied in the business of finding himself a wife to be off journeying."

Lady Lydia smiled. "Choosing one's soulmate in life should surely be an enjoyable occupation, Lord Randal. Yet you make it sound as if the Duke is approaching the matter with the serious concentration of one engaged in a military campaign. As if his very life depended upon it."

"His life may not depend on it, but his title and fortune most surely do," laughed Lord Randal. "The old Duke, his uncle, strongly disapproved of his nephew's traveling and, er, somewhat, how shall I put it, *carefree* style of living all over Europe. So he made it a condition of his will that when his nephew inherited the title, he must marry within six months. Otherwise the title is forfeited."

Stunned at this revelation, Charlotte sat open-mouthed until a blistering stare from her mother encouraged her to assume a more ladylike expression of polite indifference.

"Well," murmured Lady Lydia faintly. "How very interesting, Lord Randal. We are expecting the Duke to call on us, you know, any day now."

"I am convinced he will be delighted to make the acquaintance of you all," said Lord Randal.

Charlotte modestly lowered her eyes and Lord Randal's smile swept across her, until his eyes met Davinia's for a long, laughing moment.

Then he went on, "Since we are discussing the Duke, this seems an appropriate moment to mention a little supper party I am holding shortly. I expect my cousin the Duke to be present and, naturally, I should be most honored, Lady Lydia, if you and your family will favor the gathering with your presence."

Lady Lydia inclined her head. "We shall look forward to the occasion with pleasure, my lord."

Lord Randal rose gracefully to his feet and commented, "What charming gardens you have here, Lady Lydia. Would you permit me to escort Miss Sinclair and Miss Davinia for a stroll across the lawns?"

"Unfortunately, poor Charlotte turned her ankle this morning and would do better to rest," said Lady Lydia smoothly. "But Davinia may surely accompany you."

Outside in the warm June sunshine, Davinia laughed, "My, what a flutter you have caused in my aunt's drawing room! They could not wait to be alone to discuss your intelligence about the Duke's urgent haste to find himself a bride."

Lord Randal scowled. "Courtesy forbade me to speak of my cousin in anything but the most honorable terms. Yet to you, Davinia, I know I may speak frankly. By Jove," he said bitterly, "I would wish the Duke to hell!"

"My lord," inquired Davinia gently, "whatever is wrong?" Her instinct, then, had proved right. There was something greatly troubling the man she loved.

He sighed heavily. "My own damned fault, I suppose. Everyone warned me not to take on my cousin at the gaming tables. The man is, after all, renowned across six countries as a professional gambler."

"Were your losses very heavy?"

"Heavy! I am practically ruined!"

"But your father, the Earl. Surely he will provide you with funds?"

"My father and I are not on the best of terms," Lord Randal admitted ruefully. "He has told me I have had my allowance for the year and he'll not advance me another penny. I have a private fortune of my own, of course, but it is tied up in trust until I am twenty-five."

Davinia's heart felt like lead. That such a misfortune should strike just when everything appeared so favorable for herself and Lord Randal.

"The Duke of Strathavon should be ashamed of himself!" she flared. "Taking money from his own blood relative, his own kin. Tell me, did he win by fair means, or is he a cardsharper?"

"I must own, he is totally honest in his play," said Lord Randal. "He won't hold with Greeking. No, it was just a totally disastrous evening. I played well. Damned well. But he was brilliant. I kept raising my bids, convinced that eventually his luck would change. But, as dawn broke, I realized that bankruptcy was staring me in the face. He was decent enough to take my note for the money I owed him. Told me I could pay him anytime in the next three months. Hang it!" His fist smashed against the back of a garden seat. "How I wish I'd never set foot in that cursed gaming house!"

Seeing him so overcome, the worried Davinia deemed it best to remain tactfully silent for a while. They strolled round the paths, and for several minutes the only sound was that of the bees, humming in the fragrant rose bushes.

At last Davinia ventured, "Did the Duke not give you a sporting opportunity to win back your money?"

Lord Randal shuddered. "Ah, there my sorry tale goes from bad to worse. We rode down together from London to Bath. My cousin suggested that we stop overnight at the Pelican Inn, just west of Newbury."

Davinia froze. The Pelican Inn was a notorious haunt not only for gambling sharks, but loose women also. Oh, how she despised the Duke for encouraging Lord Randal to tarry at such a place!

"I suppose," sighed Davinia, "you lost even more money at the Pelican?"

Lord Randal nodded. "I hope . . . I trust you do not think less of me for this escapade, Davinia. I know I have been foolhardy. But your high opinion means a great deal to me."

Davinia gazed warmly into his distressed blue eyes. "I could not think less of *you*, my lord. It is the Duke of Strathavon who incurs my wrath and disfavor. It is he, plainly, who has lured you into bad company. I assure you, it would give me the greatest pleasure to see him walk up the aisle with my cousin Charlotte, for then I would know he was receiving his just deserts!"

Lord Randal let out a shout of laughter. "Davinia, you are such a tonic for my jaded spirits. So you think your cousin will be setting her cap for the Duke?"

"I am convinced of it," replied Davinia. "Tell me, what are his true feelings about the terms of his uncle's will?"

"He is furious, but resigned," said Lord Randal. "I imagine he will opt for the most convenient match possible, tie the knot, install his bride at Avonley Chantry and arrange to spend most of his time in London."

"Really?" mused Davinia. "Then I must devise some way to make Charlotte the most attractive proposition for him."

Lord Randal grimaced. "I mean no disrespect to your cousin, Davinia. But I imagine you will have a hard time convincing the Duke—and all the other eligible ladies in the county—that it is his destiny to marry Miss Sinclair."

Davinia stopped short in her tracks, her face alight. "Destiny! Yes, there lies the answer! My lord, when is your supper party for the Duke?"

"Why, I had thought a week hence."

Davinia's sea-green eyes sparkled. "Then listen to my plan! ..."

Two days later, the Duke of Strathavon paid his eagerly awaited call on the Sinclairs. At the urging of his wife, Sir William abandoned his books and dutifully seated himself in the drawing room, along with an ashen-faced Lady Lydia and a nervously excited Charlotte. Sir William expressed surprise at the absence of his niece. Lady Lydia explained, in the tense moments before the Duke's entrance, that Davinia was suffering from a headache, and was, regretfully, resting for the afternoon.

Davinia was only too glad to shut herself in her chamber for the duration of the loathsome Duke's visit. Although she was forced to admit, as she peeped from the damask window hangings, that he formed an extremely imposing figure on his magnificent gray as he rode up the drive.

He was immaculately dressed in a black cutaway coat, with white breeches and burnished top boots. As he dismounted Davinia saw a lock of blue-black hair fall carelessly over the scar on his brow.

The scar fascinated her. Could it be, she wondered hopefully, that the arrogant Duke had taken on more than he could handle in a duel of some kind, and had come off a distinct second best? She resolved to ask Lord Randal about it at the first opportunity.

As she regarded the Duke, Davinia could not suppress a fresh spurt of anger and hatred toward him. She was still smarting from his unwarranted rudeness toward her that day in the apple orchard at Avonley Chantry. As if that indignity was not enough, he had now hurled an enormous obstacle in the path of her promising romance with Lord Randal.

With all her heart Davinia cursed the Duke for encouraging Lord Randal to gamble so heavily at the tables. If the Duke had any sense of responsibility and kindness, Davinia fumed, he would have halted the game when it was clear that his cousin was on a losing streak. To allow the gaming to continue until dawn broke, and Lord Randal was ruined, struck Davinia as callous and ruthless in the extreme.

Ruthless. Yes, she thought furiously, that was the very word, the *only* word for the dark-haired Duke.

Then a sudden smile illuminated her pretty face. Well, my arrogant lord, you may be unaware, but you have met your match in Davinia Sinclair. I may not have deceived you for one instant when I pretended to be a milkmaid. That was definitely full score to you. Yet I am not defeated as easily as that. I *shall* pull the wool over your eyes and what's more, in the process, I shall promote Charlotte's cause. I shall see you wed to her yet. And in the meantime, how I am looking forward to Lord Randal's supper party!

Davinia seated herself at her small satinwood writing table and began to draw up a list of items she required for the evening of the supper party: a black velvet hat, veiling, a large square of colored silk, and *gloves*. This last item was underlined three times.

With a sigh, she laid down her quill. She would, she realized, have to exercise a considerable amount of ingenuity in obtaining these requisites. For she certainly could not afford to purchase them. She had no money. And Lady Lydia, for all her vague airs, was scrupulous about studying all bills before they were passed to Sir William for payment. Certainly the last thing Davinia desired was an inquest from Lady Lydia on why she had been squandering money on velvet hats and veiling.

Finance, or lack of it, seems to be the root of all my problems, mused Davinia. I have no money of my own and must resign myself to a practically penniless existence. Lord Randal, too, is in desperate straits, thanks to that vile Duke.

And certainly, there is no hope of Lord Randal's father, the Earl, allowing me to marry into the family whilst his son has such enormous debts. If only I were a rich heiress! Then no doubt the Earl would welcome me with open arms. But as matters stand, it is essential that Lord Randal should find himself in funds again—and soon.

What concerned Davinia was that Lord Randal had announced his intention of residing in Bath only for the summer. Then he would return to London. Once there, Davinia had nightmare visions of him becoming enmeshed by the practiced charms of any one of a score of pretty, rich young girls. Whilst Davinia would be left behind in Bath, alone and forgotten.

However, Lord Randal had declared that he was not quite cast into the Slough of Despond over his problems. Before he and Davinia had come in from the garden to join the other ladies, he had confided:

"All is not quite lost yet, Davinia. There is one glimmer of hope on the horizon. I must spend a few days completing some investigations. But when we next meet, I confidently anticipate that I shall have some more promising news about my financial situation."

"You know you may rely on me to help you, if I possibly can," Davinia had told him.

He had smiled, and pressed her hand. "Davinia, this is neither the time nor the place. But . . . I am so very fond of you, as I am sure you know. If I can only find a way to resolve my present difficulties, then have I your permission to address you again . . . on a more serious, personal level?"

Davinia was trembling with joy. His words were like a love song to her. "I shall be waiting, my lord," she had breathed.

Oh, Lord Randal, Davinia sighed now, carefully slipping her neatly written list out of sight in a drawer. What is to become of us?

Downstairs, she heard Jarvis ordering the groom to bring round the Duke's gray. Davinia found herself drawn once more to her chamber window to watch him depart. How maddening, how infuriating that her destiny lay in the hands of the commanding figure cantering confidently away down the drive.

She laughed softly. Destiny! What a strange word for her to use in connection with the Duke. For had not the gypsy indicated that her future was with Lord Randal? Davinia's spirits lifted at the thought. It was foolish, perhaps, for her to set so much store by the words of a gypsy at the fair. Some would say it was like clutching at straws in the wind.

But, at the moment, Davinia realized, that is all the hope I have to cling to.

Davinia was eager to establish whether Charlotte had made a favorable first impression on the Duke. Fired with curiosity, she ran down the stairs, remembering to moderate her steps to a leisurely pace before entering the drawing room. She was confident that Charlotte would be eager to recount every detail of the Duke's call.

She found Lady Lydia reclining full length on the sofa, overcome by the strain of the occasion. Sir William, predictably, had shut himself away in the library.

Charlotte was furiously unpicking her embroidery. As Davinia entered, she flung the sampler into her cousin's hands. "There, you help me with it, Davinia! I was in such a quake when the Duke was here, all my stitches are huge and uneven. I only pray he did not notice!"

Davinia good-naturedly began to set the sampler to rights. As she worked, she reflected wryly that judging by her own brief encounter with the Duke, she could not imagine him to be the kind of man who would overly concern himself with the niceties of embroidery stitches.

"And was your opinion of the Duke favorable, Charlotte?" she inquired.

Charlotte flushed. "Oh, he is quite formidable, Davinia. Well-mannered, and civil, of course. But, well, he has such an authoritative air about him. I confess I felt myself quite crushed. I could not think of a single word to say to him."

"You need have no fear," murmured Lady Lydia from the sofa. "You conducted yourself admirably. It was not your place to sit chattering and uttering opinions in the manner of some pert, ill-bred girl. It was quite proper that we should leave most of the conversation to your father. In fact, the Duke seemed most interested in your father's explanation of why the wheat harvests of Europe have failed so dismally in the past few years."

72

Davinia kept her attention firmly on her embroidery. Dear me, the poor Duke, she thought, her eyes brimming with mirth. What a tedious hour he must have spent! With Sir William holding forth about wheat harvests, Lady Lydia looking ready to collapse with fatigue, and Charlotte sitting simpering over the top of her ragged embroidery!

Davinia glanced up to find her aunt regarding her sternly. "I must confess, Niece, I was extremely surprised when the Duke inquired after you."

Davinia's thread broke. "*I*, Aunt Lydia?"

"Yes, you, Davinia. It seems you are already acquainted with the Duke?"

Davinia blushed poppy red. Oh, that hateful man! He had come striding into this drawing room, and evidently told her aunt about that embarrassing scene in the apple orchard. How *could* he!

"I understand," went on Lady Lydia icily, "that you had an unfortunate encounter with the blacksmith's *cow!*"

"It . . . it was all a m-misunderstanding," faltered Davinia. How much had the Duke divulged? What should she say? Really, she fumed, I loathe and detest that man more and more each passing minute!

"I declare, Mama, I rather sympathize with Davinia over the matter," said Charlotte unexpectedly. "If a cow broke loose and chased *me* down the village street, I should have hysterics. It was really very gallant of the Duke to come to Davinia's rescue, and capture the animal and leave my cousin free to walk on unmolested." She giggled. "How silly you must have looked, Davinia! Chased by a cow! How I should love to have seen you!"

Dizzy with relief, Davinia summoned a weak

73

smile. So he had not given her away after all. What an unpredictable person he was. "Indeed, it was an extremely harrowing episode," she murmured.

Lady Lydia was not satisfied. "It is yet another example of the way in which you bring nothing but discredit on the family name, Davinia. Of all the girls in the world, it would have to be *you* who was caught in such an unseemly public situation."

"I beg your pardon, Aunt."

"I hope sincerely you did not behave in too bold a fashion with the Duke. You have such an unladylike way, Davinia, of putting yourself forward. There is no meekness in your character."

Davinia considered that, on the contrary, she was displaying admirable restraint by the mild manner in which she accepted this rebuke.

Charlotte pouted. "What I cannot understand is why you did not tell us you were acquainted with the Duke?"

Why indeed? Davinia's mind raced, and her quick wits came to her rescue. "I had hoped the matter would never come to light, since I knew my aunt would be displeased by the incident."

"Your sins will always find you out, Davinia. You can be confident of that," declared Lady Lydia.

Charlotte was growing restive at Davinia's being the center of attention. "I am longing to be invited to Avonley Chantry when the Duke has completed his renovations. I should adore to see inside the house. It is said to be quite magnificent."

It is, Davinia silently agreed. Many times had she wandered round Avonley Chantry with her sketchbook. There was never anyone there to halt or challenge her. She had come to love the rambling

Elizabethan manor house, with its fine wood paneling, the priceless tapestries, the minstrels' gallery and elegant serene rooms with such wonderful views over the surrounding parkland. Even in its sad state of disrepair, the house still held an air of mellow tranquility to which Davinia had always responded. But of course, with the new Duke in residence, she was no longer at liberty to roam freely through his ancestral home.

From the faraway expression on Charlotte's face, it was clear that she was imagining herself as mistress of Avonley Chantry. The Duchess of Strathavon, wealthy, admired and envied.

Then Charlotte's brown eyes clouded. In a small, hesitant voice she inquired, "Do you think the Duke liked me, Mama?"

"Naturally, he found you charming," her mother declared soothingly. "And you will be meeting him again, shortly, at Lord Randal's supper party."

"But every girl under twenty-five will be tipping her cap at the Duke," wailed Charlotte. "Why should he choose me?"

This was the problem which was also bothering Davinia. Why, indeed, should the most eligible bachelor in all southern England choose the simpering, whey-faced Charlotte for his bride? Somehow, he must be given a strong incentive for tying the knot with Charlotte. She must be seen to possess a strong advantage over the curly-haired competition. But what?

Davinia was extremely quiet all through dinner that evening. Then, before she retired, she waited on her uncle in the library. He was seated in his favorite leather armchair, absorbed in a book on classical naval strategies.

Quietly, she poured some brandy into his near-empty glass, and brought a stool to sit by his feet. Patiently, she waited in silence, reflecting that never had she known a man with such a thirst for knowledge. Whatever the subject—from Elizabethan chimneys to Hampshire wheat harvests, her uncle wanted to know more about it.

Sir William closed the book with a smile. "What a tactful girl you are, Davinia. There is nothing worse than being interrupted in the middle of an interesting chapter. Now, what did you wish to talk to me about?"

"Charlotte, Uncle. If you remember, you mentioned to me your concern that she is not yet married."

He nodded. "I gather she is all of a flutter about the Duke of Strathavon. Most amiable man. Quite a cut above his miserly uncle."

Davinia discreetly kept her opinion of the Duke to herself. "If it could be arranged, it would indeed be an excellent match for Charlotte. But she will have to face some strong competition from all the other unmarried girls in the county. Unless, that is, we can provide the Duke with a strong incentive for marrying Charlotte."

Sir William's eyes twinkled. "What had you in mind, my clever niece?"

"The hundred acres, Uncle."

"The hundred acres! But Davinia, I have declared publicly that I will never sell that land to a Strathavon. Not after the old Duke made such an infernal fuss over the price when I was in a mood to let him buy it. No, Niece, all Bath knows I will not sell the hundred acres to a Strathavon and I cannot go back on my word."

"But if you *gave* the hundred acres as part of Charlotte's dowry, Uncle, then no one could accuse you of going back on your word, and selling it. And as the new Duke is a passionate fisherman, I am sure he will be eager to have the land as part of his estate. Did you not tell me that the hundred acres contains a loop of the River Avon?"

Sir William contemplatively sipped his brandy. "You know, I do believe you've hit on something, Davinia. It must be infuriating for the Duke to have the River Avon, and all that splendid fishing, right on his doorstep . . . yet he cannot cast a single line because that stretch of land belongs to me! I shall certainly give some serious thought to this scheme of yours, my dear. But first we must insure that the Duke finds Charlotte agreeable."

"Oh, I am convinced he does," smiled Davinia. And if my plans succeed at Lord Randal's supper party, there is no doubt that the odious Duke will find my cousin a most attractive proposition indeed!

"I declare, Miss Davinia, I don't know whether I'm coming or going, and that's the truth." Annie, Charlotte's long-suffering maid, was emerging from her mistress's room clutching an armful of dresses.

"I suppose Miss Sinclair is unable to decide which dress to wear to Lord Randal's," murmured Davinia sympathetically.

Annie nodded. "First she wants to wear the blue muslin. But no, the waist is too low on that. Then she wavers between the two new Indian muslins. But they are rejected because Miss Sinclair remembers Lady Imogen Delvigne visiting the same modiste in Bath, and Miss Sinclair is afraid the other lady will be dressed in an identical gown."

"What about the embroidered pink?" suggested Davinia helpfully.

"I think Miss Sinclair looks a picture in that," agreed Annie, "but she is worried that the lace isn't first quality. So I am to spend my morning sewing on new lace round the neck and sleeves and Miss Sinclair will make up her mind on the matter this afternoon."

Sir William, passing by, caught the tail end of this conversation and shook his head in amazement. "My, what a glum atmosphere there is about this house! I should have thought the prospect of the supper party and choosing your dresses would have brought a smile to any lady's face. Yet to listen to you one would imagine you are selecting your battle dresses, ready to march off to war."

That is not so far from the truth, mused Davinia. For in the presence of the Duke, all the unmarried girls and their mamas will be arming themselves with their most winning smiles, ready to glide into the attack.

When Sir William was out of earshot, Annie said reflectively, "He's right, Miss. There is a gloomy atmosphere about this house. Has been for the last ten years now I come to think of it." She sighed. "My, how different it was when young Master Lucien was alive."

The young man referred to was, Davinia knew, the late Lucien Sinclair, Sir William's son and heir. Tragically, he had died a day after his seventeenth birthday, of a sudden chill.

The family was so deeply grieved and shocked that even now Lucien was very rarely spoken of. But Davinia suspected that his untimely death was the reason why Lady Lydia insisted on mollycoddling her sole remaining child.

Davinia was curious to know more about Lucien, and encouraged Annie to talk. "I hear he was a very bright, lively lad."

Annie smiled. "Oh yes, Miss. He loved the outdoors and was out in even the most drenching rain, galloping around on his chestnut pony. I suppose that's how he caught the chill which led to his death. And, though it seems hard to believe now, there were such gay parties in the evenings. Why, even her ladyship would join in the fun of the charades he organized."

"His death must have been a terrible blow to her," murmured Davinia.

"Yes, both she and Sir William seemed to withdraw into themselves. They—" A bell tinkled. "Oh, excuse me, Miss. That will be Miss Sinclair ringing for me. And I haven't even started on the lace yet!"

"One moment, Annie," said Davinia hurriedly. "You mentioned charades. What did the family use for their costumes?"

"There was a big dressing-up box in the schoolroom, Miss. I wouldn't know if it's still there. No one has ventured into that part of the house since Miss Sinclair had her coming out."

The bell tinkled again, urgently this time, and Annie rushed away to attend to her mistress. Davinia ran downstairs to find Jarvis. Yes, the reliable steward had the key to the schoolroom.

"If my memory serves me right, Miss Davinia, the dressing-up trunk you ask about is in the corner furthest away from the windows."

Davinia thanked him and made her way up to the top floor of the west wing. Unlocking the schoolroom door, she found herself in a musty, airless place whose ceiling was festooned with cobwebs.

She smiled as she observed the ink-stained table, imagining a reluctant Charlotte sitting at her lessons. Lucien, too, had studied here before her, for there carved on the back of the chair were the boy's initials: *LRS*.

In the corner was the big black trunk, covered with dust. The heavy lid creaked as Davinia slowly pushed it up. But what a treasure trove she found within! Brightly colored scarves, ribbons, gauzy veils and hats of every description. Sheets knotted into Roman togas, a witch's cloak and pointed hat, a Turkish dancer's costume and an elaborate velvet gown with deep, square-cut neck—for an Elizabethan lady, perhaps? Oh, what fun they must have had, Davinia smiled.

At last, almost at the bottom of the trunk, she found what she was seeking—a simple, plain black dress. It was cut too full in the skirt, and the sleeves, also, were extravagantly voluminous. But I can deal with that, thought Davinia.

She selected some further small items from the trunk. Then she locked the schoolroom door, and clutching her black bundle, ran back to her chamber, where she reached for her sewing basket.

While she stitched, her thoughts flew as fast as her fingers . . . planning her little entertainment for the supper party . . . dreaming of Charlotte's wedding . . . and then her own.

Five

"My dear Lady Lydia, how delightful to see you again," Lord Randal bowed. "And the charming Miss Sinclair. I am honored to welcome you at my little gathering."

Lady Lydia smiled. "We have been anticipating the event with much pleasure, Lord Randal. And what a perfect setting this elegant room provides."

The main salon in the Great Pulteney Street house was decorated in Wedgwood blue. The window hangings were in a deeper shade of blue silk, whilst the marble fireplace and its white plaster reliefs provided a note of cool contrast.

Over the top of her fan, Lady Lydia surveyed the room, her long-lashed eyes missing nothing . . . sportsman Sir Richard Irwin had grown his hair a little longer to conceal his bald patch . . . Lady

Selina Delvigne resembled a peg-puff in an absurdly young, flowing gown bedecked with yellow ribbons. . . . Her daughter Imogen, however, was looking large and matronly in plum-colored silk with ruches across the bosom.

"I bring apologies," Lady Lydia told Lord Randal, "from Sir William and my niece, Davinia. My husband, I regret to say, injured his back whilst bowling this morning. It is nothing serious, but he has been ordered by his physician to rest for a few days. And my niece is unfortunately suffering from a severe headache. She begs to be excused from your gathering."

Lord Randal's handsome face assumed an expression of concern, which he noted was not mirrored on Charlotte's countenance. He had no doubt that Charlotte was well satisfied that her cousin was unable to accompany her.

He murmured, "I trust you will convey my regret at not having the pleasure of Sir William and Miss Davinia's company. I wish them both a speedy recovery."

Lady Lydia regally inclined her head. She was longing to sit down. Espying a vacant sofa, she drifted purposefully toward it with Charlotte (dressed in the embroidered pink muslin) trailing behind her. Unfortunately, Lady Selina was also approaching the sofa, from the opposite direction.

"What a charming gown, Lady Selina," murmured Lady Lydia, her hand resting covetously on the arm of the sofa. "I declare it is years since I saw so many yards of fine material all fashioned into the skirt . . . what ingenious workmanship!"

Lady Selina preened. "I confess I have no time for the skimpy dresses favored by the ladies of fashion today. This sweeping style is so graceful, is it not, and I am quite delighted with the yellow ribbons. One must adapt to the current fashion, of course, but I remember with such longing the splendid hooped gowns my grandmother wore."

"Personally, I favor the present-day mode," demurred Lady Lydia. "In years gone by, cocooned in all those swaths of material and imprisoned by hoops, one had no choice but to perch on the edge of a chair. Yet, now that the fashion is for dresses of a classical, Grecian line, it is so much easier for one to *recline*."

As she spoke, she lowered herself onto the sofa and smiled at Lady Selina in triumph. Although the sofa was large enough to accommodate two, there was of course no question of Lady Lydia moving an inch to make room for Lady Selina.

Charlotte's sharp eyes were elsewhere. Accepting a glass of wine from a footman, she murmured, "Mama, who is that strange woman in black, seated at the far end of the salon?"

With a considerable effort, Lady Lydia raised her head. The heavily veiled woman was dressed from head to toe in black, and was seated at a card table, across which had been spread a square of red silk. Paying no attention to the laughter and conversation in the salon, she sat with downcast eyes studying the pack of cards held in her gloved hands.

"Ah, you have observed my special guest," smiled Lord Randal, pausing by the ladies.

"We are highly intrigued," admitted Lady Selina. "Who is the lady, Lord Randal?"

"Her name is Madame Dresson," he informed them. "She is gifted with quite extraordinary powers.

Through the cards she is holding in her hands, she is able to see into your soul, and thence into your future."

"You mean she is a common fortuneteller," said Charlotte disdainfully.

"Most certainly not!" Lord Randal looked shocked. "You see," he lowered his voice confidentially, compelling the ladies to lean forward in order to catch his next words, "they are not ordinary playing cards she holds. They are Tarot cards."

"Tarot? What is that? I have certainly never heard of it," sniffed Charlotte.

Lord Randal smiled mystically. "Tarot cards date from far-gone medieval days. They are in fact the forerunners of our present-day deck. But instead of the suits as we know them—hearts, diamonds, etcetera—the Tarot employs cups, coins, swords and batons as symbols. In addition, there are twenty-two mysterious picture cards with intriguing titles like *Wheel of Fortune, The Magician, Death* and *The Hanged Man.*"

Lady Lydia shuddered. "Really . . . it all sounds . . . well, not quite nice."

"In the wrong hands, Lady Lydia," said Lord Randal gravely, "the Tarot can be directed to cast evil spells. In olden days, it was much associated with witchcraft and sorcery."

"Are you telling me . . ." Lady Selina was so horrified her voice disintegrated into a croak. She sipped some wine and continued, "Are you saying, Lord Randal, that that creature in black is a witch who intends casting a spell over us all?"

"Not at all, my dear Lady Selina. Pray do not alarm yourself. It was only in days gone by that the Tarot was used for ill. Then for many centuries the art of interpreting the cards was lost in the

84

mists of time. Now, there are only a few gifted people scattered round Europe who understand the mysteries of these cards. These rare souls use their powers not to cast evil spells, but to help others . . . to clarify the future, remove doubts about possible decisions, and to analyze character. All this is possible with the Tarot."

"And may I inquire," said Charlotte curiously, "where you made the acquaintance of this Madame Dresson? She is certainly not a familiar figure in Bath."

Lord Randal waved a vague hand. "We met recently in London. I discovered that Madame Dresson was born in England, and endured an unhappy marriage to a Frenchman. She is now widowed, and lives quietly in the capital. I consider myself extremely fortunate and privileged that I persuaded her to grace my little supper party here this evening."

"And are we all, then," inquired Lady Lydia distantly, "to come under the scrutiny of Madame Dresson and her Tarot cards?"

"I regret, that is impossible." Lord Randal smoothed an invisible crease from his peacock-blue waistcoat. "The reading of the Tarot cards is an intricate, mystical affair. It takes time, and intense concentration. I would not wish to impose too great a strain on Madame Dresson. But she will, I am sure, be pleased to see into the futures of a few, a special chosen few, of my guests."

Observing the doubtful expressions on the ladies' faces, Lord Randal continued blandly. "I assure you, Madame Dresson is everywhere received. In fact," once more he lowered his voice, "she will never forgive me for divulging this, but I understand that she has been invited to read the

Tarot cards in private audience for many of the crowned heads of Europe!"

He had struck just the right chord. Seeing Imogen Delvigne draw breath to speak, Charlotte cut in eagerly, "I should very much like an audience with Madame Dresson. Would you . . . do you think she would honor me with a reading?"

Lord Randal bowed. "I shall be delighted to approach her on your behalf. Meanwhile, my musicians are ready to entertain you. And I hope you will be tempted by the repast awaiting you in the supper room. Now, if you will excuse me, I believe the Duke of Strathavon has arrived. . . . "

Already the salon was buzzing with interest and speculation. Everyone was intrigued by the veiled Madame Dresson, the solitary figure still musing over her Tarot cards. And now the Duke of Strathavon himself was entering the salon, prompting the inevitable question: Would it not be fascinating if Madame Dresson could be persuaded to read the cards for the Duke?

"Why, everyone knows he is committed to finding himself a wife within six months," remarked Lady Selina. "I wonder if Madame Dresson will see his bride in the cards?"

The Duke of Strathavon's tall, commanding figure was soon the center of an attentive group. He seemed completely at ease, apparently quite unaware of both the admiring glances cast upon him by all the ladies, and the envious glares of many a young buck.

Sir Richard Irwin, the florid-faced Master of the County Hunt, inquired if the Duke would be pleased to ride with them during the season.

"Indeed, yes, I hear excellent reports of the Somerset Hunt," the Duke replied civilly.

"Sir Richard's Hunt Ball is quite the event of the year," twittered Lady Selina. "Such a feast of delicacies for supper as you would not believe. And all presented with such grace and originality."

The Duke smiled. "But is that not a tradition of the Irwin family? I believe Sir Richard's uncle was General Sir John Irwin, Lord Lieutenant for Dublin. It is said that he once displayed on table for dessert a reproduction of the fortress of Gibraltar, complete with artillery which hurled sugarplums against the walls."

Sir Richard grinned ruefully. "Too true, my lord. It was a fancy which set Sir John back fifteen hundred pounds. Eventually he was forced to flee to France to escape his debtors."

The lady in black at the card table heard the laughter and good-natured teasing as Sir Richard concluded this anecdote. But still she did not raise her eyes.

Two hours later, any skepticism Lord Randal's guests had entertained for Madame Dresson's powers was completely dispelled.

"She told me things about myself that a stranger could not possibly know," an awed Charlotte reported. "She said that in my immediate past, she could see pearls, strewn at my feet. And it is true! For not an hour before I set out this evening, my stupid maid broke the clasp on the string of pearls I intended to wear, and they scattered all over the floor!"

This was not strictly accurate. Charlotte, growing impatient when Annie was fumbling with the clasp, had tugged at it and broken the string herself.

"And what," inquired Lady Lydia with deceptive vagueness, "did Madame Dresson have to say about your future?"

Charlotte's brown eyes glowed. "She said she saw a band of gold on my finger, before I celebrate my next birthday!"

Sir Richard Irwin, too, was impressed with the insight of the mysterious lady in black.

"Dashed rum do," he muttered, gulping down a glass of wine as he returned from the silk-covered card table. "Just yesterday morning I was out for a gallop, quite alone, when the wretched horse threw me. The doctor said I was lucky not to have broken my neck. Well, I didn't mention the fall to a soul —looks a bit off, being Master of the Hunt and all, and then getting myself thrown. Yet Madame Dresson knew about it. Even told me—in the most lady-like terms, of course—just where I was most badly bruised!"

Lord Randal nodded. "I had heard she was blessed with amazing powers. Did she . . . speak of the future at all?"

"Indeed, she predicted that I was soon to become a grandfather," beamed Sir Richard. "If that is true, then it is certainly the best news of the year." He turned to the Duke of Strathavon. "My lord, will you not have Madame Dresson read your cards? I assure you, that even if you approach her table as a disbeliever, you will come away a shaken man, yet utterly convinced of her gifts."

The Duke smiled, and was about to voice a polite refusal when Lady Selina led the clamor for him to approach Madame Dresson. "Come now, my lord. Where is your sense of adventure?"

"I promise you," smiled Lord Randal, "the Duke is always game to involve himself in anything to do with playing cards. I am persuaded he is secretly intrigued by the notion of the Tarot."

"And as Lord Randal's most distinguished guest," added Sir Richard, "no doubt Madame Dresson will consider herself slighted if you do not approach her."

In the face of so much pressure, it was impossible for the Duke to demur without appearing churlish. Lord Randal led him forward toward the veiled lady at the table.

Then with a mischievous light in his blue eyes he declared, "May I present the Duke of Strathavon, Madame Dresson. He is most anxious to know if he will fulfill the terms of his uncle's will, and marry within the next six months!"

The Duke's mouth tightened, and his face darkened with anger at his cousin's impertinent remark. Grimly, he seated himself opposite Madame Dresson, and waited.

Davinia sat with thudding heart, grateful for the veiling that obscured her face. She had slipped from Chartcombe Court and ridden down to Great Pulteney Street an hour before her aunt and cousin had left for the party.

The black dress Davinia had found at the bottom of the trunk was now altered to fit her trim figure as if it had been designed specially for her. She could, of course, have saved herself hours of intricate sewing by wearing one of her own mourning gowns. But she had rejected that notion for fear that the hawk-eyed Charlotte would recognize the dress, and then herself.

In the Wedgwood-blue salon, before the first guests arrived, she and Lord Randal had conferred on who should be selected for a reading of the

Tarot cards. And, most crucial of all, what Madame Dresson should have to reveal to them.

Charlotte, naturally, presented no problem. Davinia had witnessed the drama of the pearls when she crept past Charlotte's apartments on her way out of the house.

Lord Randal had supplied the information about Sir Richard. That morning, he had chanced upon his physician taking a glass of mineral water at the Pump Room. Aware that the doctor could be encouraged into verbal indiscretions about his patients, Lord Randal invited him home for a glass of claret. This had loosened the doctor's tongue sufficiently for him to impart the intelligence of Sir Richard Irwin's fall. Even better, for Davinia's purposes, the doctor declared he had spent an hour that morning with Sir Richard's daughter, Jemima, and had been pleased to confirm that she was indeed with child.

It had, Davinia reflected, been a simple matter convincing Charlotte and Sir Richard of her mystical powers. But, glancing nervously at the Duke's scornful face, she was uneasily aware that she would need all her wits about her to fool him.

Davinia had found the Tarot cards lying in an old, neglected box in Sir William's library. Along with it was a tattered, yellowing volume which explained the meanings of all the mysterious symbols.

As the Duke approached her table, Davinia had placed the seven selected cards she intended to use for his reading, at the top of the pack. For a strictly correct reading, the book instructed that she hand the cards to the Duke to shuffle. But she knew if she allowed him to do that, she would lose all trace of her chosen seven cards, and her carefully prepared prediction of his future would most certainly go awry.

In truth, I know very little about the Tarot, thought Davinia nervously. I only hope the Duke knows less than I!

She saw he was regarding the cards curiously. "May I examine them, Madame Dresson?"

He held out a strong, broad-palmed hand. To her horror Davinia realized he was addressing her in French!

It was a moment of double turmoil for Davinia. Her schoolroom French was adequate for her to understand what the Duke had said, but would never see her through an entire conversation with him. And no, of course, he could not be allowed to touch her cards. If he upset the order of the top seven, he would scuttle all her plans!

Coolly, she replied in English, her voice low and disguised by the trace of a French accent, "If you have no objection, my lord, I should prefer to speak in English. The French tongue, you understand, brings back painful memories of an unhappy marriage."

He nodded. "Forgive me, Madame. I would not wish to cause you distress."

"And I regret I am unable to allow you to handle the cards. There is a mystic link, you understand, between each one of them and myself. For a stranger to touch them would instantly destroy the powerful aura of the Tarot."

Allowing him no time to argue, Davinia laid out the cards, face up, in a horseshoe shape on the red silk covering the table. The Duke gazed at the cards with interest.

"Most fascinating, Madame," he murmured.

"The Tarot, of course, has been known to us since medieval times. But I observe that these cards are less than fifty years old."

Davinia blanched under her veil. How was he aware of that? Surely it could not be that he knew more about the Tarot than she did herself? Oh, how disastrous, how embarrassing if he exposed her now as an impostor!

Then to her relief, the Duke continued, "Before 1750, of course, all the Tarot trumps were named in Italian. But the titles on your cards, I notice, are given in French."

He pointed to the card nearest to him on the table: *Le Jugement*. It showed a winged angel sounding a trumpet, whilst below, graves flew open and the dead rose to answer his summons.

Davinia inclined her head. It was important that she should sustain the Duke's interest in the cards, for having captured his attention she would find it easier to convince him that what she was about to tell him was true.

"The cards belonged to my husband's *grand-mère*, my lord. It was she who recognized my gift, and kindly condescended to pass on her knowledge to me. Now, shall we begin?"

The Duke smiled sardonically. "With pleasure, Madame. Though I hardly imagine you can have anything to tell me about myself that I do not already know."

"That remains to be seen," murmured Davinia. "The first card before you, *Le Jugement*, refers to past influences in your life."

"Judgment!" laughed the Duke mockingly. "Indeed, that sounds distinctly ominous!"

"Particularly so," Davinia agreed, ignoring the taunting note in his voice, "because the picture on the card has fallen the wrong way up. It is what we call reversed. The card indicates guilt and dissatisfaction with your previous way of life, and self-reproach for all the opportunities you have wasted."

The Duke's face was quite unreadable. Which was only natural, Davinia mused, remembering that he was a gambler. He must never, even by the flicker of an eyelid, give anything away. Indeed, Davinia had heard that some gentlemen wore masks at the tables in order that their expressions of dismay or triumph would not be revealed.

Davinia was amused to notice, however, that the sardonic twist had vanished from the Duke's mouth. Had her reading struck a chord within him? She had based it on the surmise that as he had lived abroad and had a considerable reputation for wild living (and even wilder loving), he would inevitably have suffered pangs of remorse from time to time about his self-indulgent life-style.

Seeing that he was determined to make no comment, she passed on to the second card. "Ah. The *Two of Batons*. A card which relates to your present circumstances. It suggest riches and authority which you have gained by just means."

He nodded, still not prepared to look impressed. After all, one did not require mystic powers to know that he had inherited a dukedom and considerable wealth from his uncle. All England was aware of that.

"The third card," Davinia explained, "pertains to general future conditions. It is, as you see, the *Seven of Cups*. It indicates that you will be faced with several alternatives. But you are required to summon all your vision and wisdom to perceive that one of these choices is very much to your advantage over the others."

The Duke's dark lashes flickered momentarily. "This reading, Madame, is proving far more . . . subtle than I had anticipated."

"Please," ordered Davinia, holding up her gloved hand, "you will disturb the spell. Now we come to card four, which indicates the best policy for you to follow when making your choice. Ah, it is another trump card. *Temperance.*" The picture portrayed a woman pouring liquid from one vessel to another. "It suggests success in your aims, through the channels of a harmonious partnership."

Davinia paused, to allow him time to digest her words. She had selected the term *harmonious partnership* with deliberate care. The Duke's mind was, of necessity, set on thoughts of marriage. Yet how fatal it would be if he surveyed the field of pretty, eligible young ladies and allowed himself the luxury of falling in love with one of them.

Not, on serious reflection, that Davinia could imagine anyone as ruthless as the Duke indulging in such an emotional activity as falling in love. Yet, she could take no chances. Cupid's arrow was capricious and quite unpredictable. It was not unknown for the dart of Love to pierce even the most stony of hearts.

No, at all costs the Duke must not succumb to love. Instead, he must be encouraged to see the wisdom of a practical, useful alliance . . . such as that with the daughter of his neighbor, Sir William Sinclair.

Davinia continued, "The fifth card, my lord, concerns your standing in the eyes of those around you. Oh, it is a good card. The *Ace of Swords.* It indicates that people regard you as a born leader, blessed with natural authority. Now we come to the sixth card, which is important because it points to the obstacles standing in the path of that which you seek to achieve."

Davinia was now working toward the climax of her carefully rehearsed performance. Sir William, she knew, would shortly let it be known (in the most roundabout, gentlemanly manner) that if the Duke were to offer for Charlotte's hand, then he would give her, as part of her dowry, the one hundred acres coveted so long by generations of Strathavons.

"The card is the *Ten of Coins*," murmured Davinia. "And see, it is reversed. It points to the restricting effects of a long custom or tradition. An ancient feud, perhaps, is involved. Although you yourself were not one of the original participants, the repercussions of this ill-feeling still adversely affect you."

Surely, Davinia thought, the Duke must have grasped by now that I am referring to the Strathavon /Sinclair feud over the hundred acres. Short of shouting it from the rooftops, I can make it no plainer!

The Duke was staring at Davinia now, his expression intense and unfathomable. Davinia shivered, convinced that his brilliant blue eyes were boring right through the disguise of her veil.

"Pray continue, Madame," he urged quietly.

"We have reached the final. the all-important card," Davinia declared. "It indicates the probable outcome of your quest. You will observe, my lord, that the card is the *Two of Cups*. It appears that the Fates are to be kind to you. The card suggests joyous harmony and reconciliation. I see a treaty signed . . . a dowry perhaps? Certainly, the end of a feud, and the resolving of arguments into mutual cooperation."

Davinia sat back in her chair, feeling suddenly

fatigued. She studied the Duke's rugged face carefully, searching for some sign that she had indeed outwitted him.

He smiled. "You have given me much to dwell upon, Madame. I confess, I am quite captivated by the Tarot cards. Tell me, are you familiar with the game Tarocco?"

"Whatever is that, my lord?" inquired Lady Selina. Curiosity had driven her across to the table, where she hoped (in vain) to hear part of Madame Dresson's reading for the Duke.

"Tarocco is one of the oldest card games still played in Europe," the Duke explained courteously. "As the Tarot cards are used for it, I wondered if Madame Dresson would be kind enough to teach me the rudiments of the game."

Davinia had never heard of Tarocco before this moment. She gathered up the cards, and said loftily, "Naturally in France I have seen Tarocco played, many times. But I would not demean my cards by employing them in a mere game. The reading of the Tarot is an art, requiring years of serious study, my lord. Lowly card games I leave to those who have nothing better to do in life than seek empty amusement for their idle hours."

The Duke raised a surprised eyebrow and seemed on the verge of carrying the discussion further. But with Lady Selina poised to repeat his every word all over Bath, he wisely restrained himself to a polite, "I have spent a most profitable half hour in your company, Madame. After such mental exertions, you must be in dire need of refreshment. May I have the honor of escorting you to the supper room?"

Davinia was almost faint with hunger, and her

poor throat felt sorely parched. But not a morsel of food, nor drop of wine could pass her lips whilst she remained in public view. For that would involve lifting her veil, which was, of course, out of the question. Gracefully, she declined the Duke's offer.

Before he could press her further, Lord Randal came hurrying to the rescue. Quietly, he escorted her downstairs to a quiet salon, where Davinia collapsed onto a sofa with a sigh of relief.

"I had best not remove my veil for someone might happen upon us," she said. "But oh, my lord, I do believe our scheme succeeded!"

"The Duke certainly seems in a thoughtful mood," remarked Lord Randal. "What a feat if you have really sown the seeds in his mind that an alliance with Miss Sinclair would be the most advantageous solution to his marriage problem!"

"It was monstrous hard work," confessed Davinia. "With Sir Richard and Charlotte I was able to turn up any cards and put whatever interpretation I chose on them. But I dared not do that with the Duke. I am sure he was committing each card and everything I said to memory, and will make it his business to check with a genuine Tarot card reader whether my words were correct. I spent an age selecting the most appropriate cards for the message I wanted to make him believe." She clasped her hands, her eyes dancing. "Oh, how wonderful if I really have outwitted him! Such an arrogant, overbearing man deserves to be taken down a peg or two!"

Lord Randal was looking anxious. "I fear I must shortly return to my guests. But will you not take

97

just one glass of wine with me? I have some news for you. There is something we must discuss, most urgently."

Davinia hesitated, sorely tempted to tarry awhile with Lord Randal. But there was the ride back to Chartcombe Court still to be completed. "No, I must not delay, my lord. Lady Lydia never stays out late. She and Charlotte will be departing soon, and I must be home before them."

"I shall send one of my footmen with you. I will not allow you to ride through Bath alone at night. And when shall we meet again, Davinia?"

"Tomorrow morning?" suggested Davinia. "Charlotte is coming to meet Lady Imogen at the Pump Room, and I am to have a riding lesson."

Lord Randal smiled. "Then I too shall be out riding tomorrow. I shall be in such a fever of impatience, for I am longing to tell you my news! You will not believe your pretty ears!"

Six

Charlotte was in high spirits as she and Davinia rode into Bath the following morning.

"Such a diverting evening at Lord Randal's, Cousin. I would not have missed it for all the world. I did tell you, did I not, that Madame Dresson foretold that I would be married before my next birthday?"

"Yes, Charlotte, you have mentioned the episode." Charlotte had prattled of nothing else all morning. "Though I am surprised," Davinia went on mischievously, "that you of all people should place so much store by this strange woman's reading. After all, I recall you were extremely scornful when I had my fortune told at the fair."

"Oh, but you consulted a common gypsy," retorted Charlotte contemptuously. "Madame Dresson is a lady. A person of breeding, you understand.

She is blessed with the rare gift of being able to interpret the meaning of the Tarot cards. Why, the crowned heads of all Europe hang on her every word. And it is not as if she permitted all and sundry in the salon to approach her. Only the chosen few were called."

Davinia's sea-green eyes glimmered with amusement. "You were indeed honored, Charlotte. And she read the cards for the Duke of Strathavon too, you say? I wonder what she told him!"

"Oh, we were all of a tremble to know!" exclaimed Charlotte. "But by the time Lady Selina plucked up courage to draw near Madame Dresson's table, the reading was over. Yet, this I will tell you," Charlotte's tone was smugly triumphant, "at supper, the Duke was most attentive toward Mama and I. We conversed together for the best part of half an hour!"

Charlotte was, sadly, apt to exaggerate. After Davinia had left Lord Randal's house, Lady Lydia had insinuated herself into the group surrounding the Duke. She had then proceeded to bombard him with question after question.

How did he favor England after so many years abroad? . . . Did he not consider Bath the most delightful of cities? . . . How was the work on Avonley Chantry progressing? . . . She had heard that the manor house possessed the most charming minstrels' gallery . . . Was the Duke interested in music? . . . Dear Charlotte played and sang so beautifully, music was a positive passion with her. . . .

Finally the Duke had managed to extricate himself, and left the gathering shortly afterward.

"He is to give a ball," Charlotte said breathlessly, trotting her horse gently down the hill. "As soon as Avonley Chantry is restored. We are all invited. Oh, I can hardly wait! How dull life was before the Duke took up residence in Bath. Now there appears to be so much to look forward to!"

As they left the bustling streets of Bath and entered the Pump Room, Charlotte asked anxiously, "Cousin, do you imagine the Duke will be here this morning?"

"One never knows what the Fates have in store," murmured Davinia dryly.

Leaving Charlotte with Lady Selina and her daughter Imogen, Davinia made her way to Mr. Dash's celebrated riding school in Montpelier Row. She found Lord Randal already there, critically observing the rather undisciplined game of a couple on the nearby tennis courts.

"I have advised Mr. Dash that I shall take you out for a lesson today, Davinia," smiled Lord Randal. His blue eyes were bright in appreciation of Davinia's fresh, youthful looks, enhanced by the dark green velvet riding habit that graced her petite, feminine figure.

He went on, "My, what a delight it is to see your pretty face unveiled once more. Even I felt distinctly in awe of you as Madame Dresson! Yet what a triumph you were. Both Sir Richard Irwin and Lady Selina were eager to engage you for soirees of their own. They were quite dashed when I informed them you were leaving immediately for Spain, for an audience with the highest in the land!"

Laughing, they set off at a gentle canter along a winding path that led them out into the lush Somerset countryside. Davinia, although happy to see Lord Randal again, would have preferred to ride in silence for a while, the more to appreciate the beautiful landscape, so lovely on this sunny summer day. The trees and hedgerows were in full green leaf, and cowslips provided splashes of yellow on the verdant hillsides.

But Lord Randal, with much on his mind, had no eyes today for his glorious surroundings. "I declare, I have been counting the hours until I could converse with you alone," he said impatiently. "Rein in your horse beside that gate for a while, Davinia. Now hear this! I believe I have found a way to put myself in funds once more!"

"What do you propose to do," laughed Davinia, "hold up a stagecoach?"

"Something far more interesting than that," he smiled. "I intend that you and I should engage in a treasure hunt, Davinia."

Her eyes widened. "Treasure? Whatever do you mean Lord Randal?"

He folded his arms across his chest and told her, "I had a Great-Aunt Violetta who lived here in Bath. In her youth, she was an extremely willful young lady, and against her parents' wishes insisted on marrying a handsome, charming, though feckless, young man."

"Why were her parents against this marriage?" asked Davinia.

"Because they knew so little about Roland, or his family. He hailed from somewhere up north, I believe. Also, Violetta's father suspected that Roland was merely marrying Violetta for her money. She was an extremely wealthy woman in her own right."

"But what has this to do with treasure?" asked Davinia, intrigued.

Lord Randal raised a finger. "Be patient. I am giving you the background to the situation. Well, Violetta was married barely a month before she discovered that her parents were right. Roland was an inveterate gambler and night after night he could be observed in the gaming clubs, squandering his wife's fortune. He also drank very heavily, and Violetta had nightmares of being left a penniless widow, totally unprovided for."

"She has all my sympathy," sighed Davinia.

"After two years of marriage, all Violetta had left were her jewels. They were renowned throughout southern England . . . a fortune in emeralds, sapphires and diamonds. A quite magnificent collection."

"But when her husband had exhausted all the available money, surely he would have insisted on selling her jewels to finance his gambling," commented Davinia shrewdly.

"This was exactly what Violetta feared. Though strangely enough, despite all his faults, she still loved Roland. Would never hear a word said against him."

"You did say he was handsome and charming," smiled Davinia.

"Mmm, well, he certainly seems to have cast a spell over Violetta. Yet she had the sense to realize that she must hide the jewels from him, as security for her future. That was speedily done."

"Where did she conceal them?" asked Davinia.

Lord Randal sighed. "Ah, the crucial question. I am coming to that. The inevitable happened. Roland ran through all the cash, and instructed her to sell some of her jewels. Violetta faced him, and confessed that she had hidden the valuables. I imagine Roland must have been furious. Yet, as I said, he was capable of charming the birds from the trees."

"So he set about persuading her to reveal the whereabouts of the gems," said Davinia.

"He did indeed. After a while, Violetta could feel herself weakening. He must really have come the blarney over her. Then, as a last desperate hope, she decided to appeal to his adventuring instincts. She told him the jewels were his—if he could find them. And she set him a riddle."

"That was clever," said Davinia admiringly. "At least it gave her a breathing space whilst he unraveled the clues."

"He never did untangle the clues," said Lord Randal. "Both he and Violetta were carried off by smallpox not long afterward."

"Poor Violetta," sighed Davinia. "From your description, I feel I know her so well. But what happened to her jewelry?"

"It remains hidden," replied Lord Randal. "You see, the only person who knew the whole story of the gems and riddle was Violetta's elder sister. When she died, she imparted the information to her faithful housekeeper, who then came to live in my father's household. I remember the housekeeper telling me the tale as a child, but I paid scant attention to it then. I have never before found myself short of funds. And, I confess, I was too idle to go chasing about Bath following up clues to riddles."

Davinia was utterly enthralled by the story. "The clues, Lord Randal. What became of them?"

"They were mixed up with all Violetta's letters and personal papers in an old box up in the attic of my father's London house. That is why I was unable to reveal to you, until now, what I had in mind. I knew I had to gain possession of that box, and find the clues."

"And did you?" cried Davinia.

He nodded, his words coming quickly, "I sent

my man to the house with a note asking my father if he would allow me to have the box. Fortunately, the old boy was in a good humor, and agreed. It arrived yesterday. And," he drew a hand into his riding coat, "here are the clues, my lovely Davinia, written in Violetta's own fair hand."

Breathless with anticipation, Davinia took the piece of yellowed parchment. The old-fashioned writing was not easy to decipher, but after a few minutes Davinia was able to make sense of the closely written lines. She read aloud:

My first is of marble, so pure and so white,
I forbade a Princess to dance through midnight!

My second has stood o'er a thousand proud years,
Since a Mercian King dewed the site with his tears.

To my third, unlike Royalty, I never roam,
Yet it seems as familiar as my own home.

To the shadows of four many ladies would steal,
For to dance but a step was a blushing ordeal.

Round my fifth horses trot—not common or low,
'Tis elegant here—not a traveling show!

My sixth is the color of love strong and true,
The flower of one, dear, closest to you.

My last in shape is almost where I be,
And the name of the monarch who shelters me.

To find my whole toss the letters in the air,
'Tis a splendid place—but enter if you dare!

"What is your opinion?" Lord Randal inquired anxiously as Davinia lifted her eyes from the parchment.

"Poor Roland," she laughed. "I declare, had he lived he would have tied himself in knots attempting to unravel those clues."

"It makes no sense to me," confessed Lord Randal. "What does it mean: *To find my whole toss the letters in the air?* Which letters?"

"Ah, I have seen this sort of riddle before," Davinia reassured him. "The secret is to find the answer to each individual clue. Then take the initial letter of each of your seven answers. Jumble them up and that, in theory, is this splendid place which Violetta suggests Roland was nervous of entering. I wonder why?"

Lord Randal shook his head. "I wish I knew more about Violetta. It would help us considerably, I believe, on our search. But the only people who were on intimate terms with her are dead now."

"You said *our* search, my lord," faltered Davinia. "Are we, then, to look for the treasure together?"

He grinned down at her. "I'd be monstrous glad of your help, Davinia. You have such a lively mind. And being a lady, you might be able to fathom out the direction of Violetta's thoughts when she set those clues. I've always maintained that women are far more devious creatures than men. Frankly, I haven't a notion about any of the riddle. I've studied each clue until my eyes swam, but still I'm totally in the dark."

Davinia read the riddles again, slowly this time. Then a brilliant smile illuminated her lovely face.

"Of course! Number six. *The color of love strong and true, The flower of one, dear, closest to you.* I am quite positive that violet is the shade which represents fidelity in love. And as your aunt's name was Violetta, then she would surely regard the violet as her own special flower."

Lord Randal dashed his fist against his thigh. "Confound it, why did I not think of that! Why, the answer is so simple when someone explains it to you! Violet. Good. So we have made a start. We know one letter at least. V for *Violet*. Have you any more stunning ideas, Davinia?"

Ruefully, the golden-haired girl shook her head. "I fear that is the limit of my inspiration for this morning. As you say, it is a pity we know so little about Violetta. But if I may keep the parchment, I shall reread the clues at every opportunity. I am sure to have fresh thoughts on the matter."

"I have another copy at home." Lord Randal took her hand, his boyishly handsome face suddenly serious. "I am so glad and grateful that you are helping me in this search, Davinia. It means a great deal to me, you know, to find those jewels. My whole future depends upon it. And I hope . . . I trust that your future will be linked with them also."

Davinia flushed with happiness. He could not, clearly, say any more at this stage. But his intentions were crystal clear to her. When the jewels were found, and he was in funds once more, then Lord Randal was surely determined to ask her to marry him.

With trembling fingers she gathered up the reins. Together, she and Lord Randal began to canter gently on a circular route through the hills which would bring them back into Bath.

Davinia felt like singing for joy. How sweet to be out on such a glorious summer's day, with the bees humming, the birds in full song, the scent of honeysuckle in the hedgerows—and beside her the man she loved, the man who had just given her the broadest of hints that he wanted to marry her. How good life was!

Quite unbidden, and most unwelcome, there

came then into her mind an image of the Duke of Strathavon. Davinia shook her head, trying to rid herself of such an unpleasant vision.

But of course, she sighed, it was impossible for her to dream of her own marriage without first considering Charlotte's prospects. And in that connection it was inevitable that her thoughts should stray to the Duke.

She remembered her first glimpse of him as she peered, that fateful day, through the leaves of the apple tree in his orchard. The rugged, lean face, harshly brilliant blue eyes, the sardonic twist to his lips and that curious scar on his forehead . . .

On impulse she turned to Lord Randal and remarked, "I trust your cousin the Duke enjoyed the supper party last night. Charlotte was most overwhelmed that he conversed with her and my aunt during supper."

Lord Randal laughed. "I am of the opinion that *you* gave him much food for thought, Madame Dresson!"

"If not a severe bout of indigestion," smiled Davinia. "Do you think he will see the merits of a match with my cousin? I fear the competition will be fierce. There is not an unattached girl in the county who is not at this moment dreaming of a duchess's tiara adorning her hair."

Lord Randal's eyes narrowed thoughtfully, "Ah, but you must mind that the Duke is a practical man. He has had many—how shall I put it—romantic liaisons with beautiful women, both here and abroad. But I have never heard tell that he has allowed any lady to capture his heart."

If, indeed, he possesses such a thing as a heart, reflected Davinia skeptically.

"As you say," went on Lord Randal, "every

giddy, simpering miss will be fawning around him, and this will bore him beyond endurance. No, if your uncle is serious about giving Miss Sinclair the hundred acres as part of her dowry, then I am convinced the Duke will speedily see the wisdom of the match. And once the knot is tied, with his inheritance secured, he will then be free to live his life in his own style, with naught else to worry him."

"Have you any notion," Davinia inquired, "how he came by that strange scar above his eyebrow?"

"I have heard tell that the incident occurred in Italy," replied Lord Randal. "The Duke entered a private gaming house and observed that a lady of his acquaintance was losing heavily against a rogue who was engaged in some outrageous sharp practice."

Davinia raised her eyes heavenward. "I might have guessed that gambling would be at the root of it!" she sighed.

Lord Randal hurried on, "No doubt the Duke's first instinct was to take on the cross-man himself. But I gather that on reflection he realized that he was too well known, and would instantly arouse the villain's suspicions. Instead, the Duke hired a stranger, another cardsharper, to challenge the blackguard at the tables. When the winnings were complete, the Duke strode across to the table, paid his hired man and handed his . . . er . . . lady friend back the money she had lost. The Greeker was so furious at being publicly dished in this fashion, he attacked the Duke with a silver dagger."

"But I was always led to believe that weapons were strictly forbidden in gaming establishments," cried Davinia.

"That is certainly the case, for the most obvious of reasons," agreed Lord Randal. "But this rogue had secreted a dagger in his boot and, as I say, lunged at the Duke, drawing blood on his forehead. The Duke recovered instantly, seized a brass candlestick and beat the man off, leaving him in a very sorry state." Lord Randal paused for a moment. "I must own, that although I myself have suffered at the hands of the Duke at the tables, he is nevertheless a straight-dealing gentleman. He will not tolerate ferreting of any description."

Davinia's blood ran suddenly cold at the notion of the Duke discovering that she had tricked him over the matter of the Tarot cards. How furious he would be! Yet, how could he possibly discover the truth, she reassured herself. It was not as if Bath were bursting at the seams with genuine Tarot readers. Indeed, the Duke had seemed utterly convinced by her performance, listening thoughtfully throughout to all she had told him.

As she and Lord Randal rode down into Bath, Davinia mused on what she had learned of the Duke's character. His handling of the cardsharper in Italy was most revealing. For he had not chosen the most obvious course of confronting the cheat himself. That way would have been most dramatic, certainly, but the rogue would most definitely have recognized him and refused to play. Then the Duke's lady friend (and who might *she* be?) would never have regained her money.

No, by employing more subtle tactics, the Duke had insured the ultimate success of his plan. Most ingenious, applauded Davinia. I must bear his strategy in mind if I am unfortunate enough to engage in further encounters with him.

Back in the city, Lord Randal accompanied Davinia to the Pump Room, where she was to meet Charlotte. As was usual in the mornings, the area was thronged with elegant Bath society, taking turns up and down the room or sitting drinking glasses of warm mineral water.

A band entertained them with all the fashionable tunes of the day. It was popular with the ladies, though many of the gentlemen, who were present for a quiet perusal of the London newspapers, complained that the musicians played far too loudly.

Charlotte, Lady Selina and Lady Imogen were seated near the great clock. Charlotte's thin shoulders were drooping.

"We have been here for hours," she declared, "but have met no one of any *consequence*."

Lord Randal murmured, "It is most delightful to see you again so soon after my little gathering, Miss Sinclair. I was most grateful to you and Lady Lydia for keeping the Duke so entertained during supper. I am convinced he greatly enjoyed his conversation with you."

"Yet he left immediately after supper," said plump Lady Imogen, pointedly.

"The Duke asked me to express his apologies," said Lord Randal smoothly. "He was obliged to rise at the crack of dawn this morning to conduct his new baliff on a tour of the Avonley Chantry estate."

Charlotte rose. "In that event, we may as well go home, Davinia."

Charlotte was, Davinia reflected wryly, nothing if not direct. As her cousin fussed around her chair, collecting her shawl and parasol, Davinia felt Lord Randal clutch at her arm.

"Look over there," he whispered excitedly.

Following his gaze, Davinia let out a small gasp. Before them was an impressive statue of a portly, important-looking man in a curled wig.

"It is fashioned of marble," breathed Davinia. "*My first is of marble, so pure and so white.* Do you imagine . . . ?"

"The first step is to determine who the statue honors," said Lord Randal.

Lady Selina had overheard. "Shame on you for not recognizing such a famous gentleman," she admonished Lord Randal. "It is Beau Nash, of course. He was a very prominant figure in Bath in my father's day."

"In what manner *prominent* Lady Selina?" inquired Davinia, smiling as she observed Mr. Nash's ample girth.

She recalled the second line of the riddle: *I forbade a Princess to dance through midnight.* Yet Mr. Nash was not a Royal. He had not even possessed a title. So how had he contrived to impose his will on a Princess?

"Amongst other things, Mr. Nash was in charge of the Assembly Rooms, as Master of Ceremonies," Lady Selina informed them. "He was extremely strict and kept everyone in order. I fear there was a considerable rowdy element in Bath at that time—local farming types mainly, with farmyard manners to match. But Mr. Nash insisted they all behave in a sober fashion. And he stopped them carousing in the streets till all hours by ending every ball at eleven o'clock prompt."

"Even," hazarded Davinia, trying a shot in the dark, "when visiting Royalty were in attendance?"

Lady Selina's eyebrows rose. "How curious that you should mention Royalty, my dear. Yes, the

Princess Amelia once attended a ball here. When the Master of Ceremonies called a halt to the revels at eleven o'clock she cried imperiously, 'one more dance, Mr. Nash. Remember, I am a Princess!' And he drew himself up and replied, 'Yes, Madam, but I reign here, and my laws must be kept!' "

"However did the Princess react?" asked a horrified Charlotte.

"At first she was speechless at his impertinence. But then she smiled sweetly, and swept from the room with her entourage. I understand that ever afterward, the Princess always spoke of Mr. Nash in the most respectful terms. Mind, she was a monstrous eccentric lady. She was fond of winter fishing on the Avon. But instead of freezing to death over her sport, she installed herself in a summer house, specially equipped with a fireplace at each end. Ah," sighed Lady Selina wistfully, "those were the days my dears . . ."

Davinia and Lord Randal walked behind the three ladies as they left the Pump Room.

"So," whispered Lord Randal, "we are making progress. We now have $N - - - - V -!$"

"It is an excellent start for our first day," agreed Davinia. "I shall give the matter all my attention henceforth."

"I shall be at church on Sunday as usual," said Lord Randal as he prepared to take his leave. "Perhaps by then we shall each have had fresh inspiration."

As he rode away down Cheap Street, Davinia felt suddenly lonely as she watched the tall, good-looking young man acknowledging acquaintances, and tipping his hat to the ladies as he passed by. How Davinia longed for the world to know of their love!

How wonderful it will be when we have found the jewels, and Lord Randal is in funds once more. Then the way will be clear for us to marry—providing of course that the Duke ties the knot with Charlotte. Surely, there is nothing I desire more in life than to be Lord Randal's bride. We shall be the happiest couple in all England. And once we are wed—

"Come, Davinia! Do you intend to stand there daydreaming forever? I have wasted an entire morning in Bath and now I wish to go home!"

Charlotte's earlier high spirits of the morning had evaporated, leaving her in the most thoroughly disagreeable temper. She would remain upset, Davinia surmised, until she was given the opportunity to converse once more with the Duke.

Davinia prayed that meeting would be soon, for Charlotte's sake. Though, personally, Davinia could not imagine anyone actually desiring to be in the Duke's company. Once more she imagined herself in the apple tree on the occasion of her first encounter with the Duke. His harsh, arrogant voice had startled her so much she had almost dropped her sketch folder right onto his head. How disastrous that would have been!

Davinia's heart missed a beat. Her sketch folder! In all the confusion, she had left it there, up in the apple tree house. Swiftly, her mind skimmed through its pages. There were some wicked caricatures—of Lady Lydia swooning on the sofa, and Charlotte kicking at the bedpost in one of her infamous tempers.

There was a portrait of her beloved Lord Randal, something she had never permitted him to see, but which comforted her in all the hours she was parted from him. Worst of all, there were drawings of the interior of Avonley Chantry. On her solitary visits to the great old Elizabethan manor house, she had sketched all her favorite places . . . the minstrels' gallery, with its age-old echoes of lute and dulcimer . . . the view across the park from the old library . . . and the magnificent Long Gallery, which contained one of the finest collections of watercolors and portraits in all England.

Davinia closed her eyes in panic at the notion of one of the Duke's servants finding her sketch folder and handing it to his master. There would be no doubt to whom it belonged, for she had signed her name on the front.

If the Duke saw it, he would know that not only had she been accustomed to trespassing on his land, but she had taken the same liberty with his house! And, thought Davinia in despair, I cannot allow him to set eyes on those astringent sketches of my aunt and cousin. Especially the one of Charlotte in a dander. That his future bride should besport herself in such an unladylike manner! Why, he might change his mind about marrying Charlotte, and then all my plans will be ruined.

And then there is my portrait of Lord Randal. I must have *that* back.

But the Duke had forbidden her to set foot on his land again. "If you come here again, I warn you, I shall personally take a horsewhip to you!" he had threatened.

Davinia flushed angrily at the memory. How dare he speak to me in that arrogant manner! I *shall* have my property back, Duke or no Duke. And if he discovers me, and lays so much as a finger on me, I'll scratch and claw and kick and bite—so he'll be left with a dozen scars on his face, not merely one!

Seven

Warily, Davinia pushed open the old iron gate that led into the Avonley Chantry grounds. She had been fearful that the Duke would have ordered a lock to be fitted to the gate as a deterrent against intruders like herself attempting to trespass on his land. But, no doubt, Davinia reflected as she ran lightly through the orchard, the lock would be one of the first tasks for the Duke's new baliff.

The grass beneath her feet was perfectly dry. Thank heavens, thought Davinia, the weather has been so clement. It would only have taken one downpour of rain to leave my poor sketch folder completely sodden and ruined.

As she approached her favorite apple tree Davinia trod softly, taking care to insure that she was alone. Fortunately, the dreaded Duke was nowhere in sight.

As always, the orchard was peaceful and tranquil, in marked contrast to the fine Elizabethan house which was a hive of noisy activity. Stonemasons, carpenters and workmen were hard at work restoring the old house to its former grandeur.

How splendid it will look when it is complete, Davinia mused. She recalled with longing the many times she had wandered through the deserted rooms of the house, sketching . . . dreaming . . . lost in contemplation of the ladies and gentlemen who had inhabited the mansion in days gone by. It was impossible to repress a pang of sorrow as she realized she would never again be able to wander there so freely. In future, she would enter the house only as a guest—as Charlotte's guest, if all her plans succeeded.

Which is how it should be, Davinia reminded herself sharply. By the time Charlotte is married to the Duke, you will have no time to feel sad about Avonley Chantry. You will be happily engaged in your own marriage arrangements, preparing to set up your household, with Lord Randal Maunsell.

Cheered by this prospect, Davinia cast one final glance around the orchard. Reassured that no one of authority was within sight, she lifted her skirt and shinned with practiced ease up the apple tree. To her relief, there was the sketch folder, lying exactly where she had left it.

Davinia was sorely tempted to linger awhile, enjoying the dappled warmth of the sun as it filtered through the fresh green leaves. But the notion of the Duke's wrath if he discovered her once again on his property sent her scurrying to the ground, and back as fast as her legs would carry her to the safety of her uncle's estate on the other side of the iron gate.

Feeling considerably elated at the success of her mission, Davinia decided to stroll down to the village. A couple of months previous she had started a sketch of the village smithy, which an April shower had forced her to abandon. Today, she decided, was the perfect time to complete her drawing.

Contentedly, she settled herself on an old tree stump opposite the smithy, and taking a piece of charcoal from her folder, set to work. The village folk were quite accustomed to pretty young Miss Davinia sitting quietly at her sketching, and she greeted them all with a cheerful wave and a smile as they passed by on their daily business.

Little red-haired Rosie, the smith's daughter, was playing with her new puppy, and soon Davinia had composed a quite delightful picture. It showed the smithy, with Mr. Jarratt hard at work at his forge, and young Rosie outside, throwing a stick for the bright-eyed Patch.

Noticing that the right-hand side of her drawing required more weight, Davinia began to sketch in a gentleman, who would be waiting for Mr. Jarratt to shoe his horse. When she had been working on the figure of the man for about ten minutes, Davinia realized with amusement and surprise that the tall, arrogant person she had drawn was modeled on none other than the Duke of Strathavon.

Well, so be it, she smiled to herself, shading the face to enhance its lean, rugged lines, and not forgetting the distinctive scar on the brow. She had caught his imposing stance perfectly, Davinia decided. The imperious stare . . . the commanding lift of the chin . . . the attitude which seemed to indicate that he was master of the entire world.

"Yes, it will do very nicely," Davinia murmured approvingly to herself.

"On the contrary. I fear the nose is a little too short," said a mocking voice behind her. "And how unobservant of you not to have noticed that I wear my signet ring on my *right* hand, not my left as you have drawn."

Davinia's smile fled as she whirled round. The Duke of Strathavon was standing, hands on hips, laughing down at her. She made a movement to snap her folder shut, but he was too swift for her. He seized the folder and held it aloft, clearly with the express purpose of examining her work.

"How dare you interfere with what does not belong to you!" cried Davinia. She was frantic in case he should see the sketch of Charlotte in an ugly temper, or the drawings portraying the interior of Avonley Chantry. "And how underhand, sneaking up behind me in such a fashion!"

As she spoke, she jumped up, hoping to snatch the folder from him. But he held it tantalizingly just out of reach.

"My dear Miss Davinia, I am delighted to see you in such good health. Only recently you have been smitten by two severe headaches which have prevented your joining us in society. I am so relieved to find you are fully recovered and, one might almost say, fighting fit!"

Davinia flushed, recalling the excuses of headaches she had given when the Duke paid his call at Chartcombe Court, and again to explain her absence at Lord Randal's supper party.

"I am surprised," declared Davinia haughtily,

attempting to recover a measure of her poise, "that you should lower yourself sufficiently even to notice my absence from any gathering."

His blue eyes held hers. "On the contrary," he murmured—but before he could continue, Rosie's puppy dashed across the road in pursuit of a ginger kitten. In the ensuing confusion, as the kitten raced up a tree, Davinia took advantage of the diversion to try to seize her folder from the Duke's grasp. She managed to tear it from him, but the sketches slipped free and fluttered into the road.

"Oh, allow me," said the Duke courteously, bending to gather up the drawings.

"Pray, do not trouble yourself . . . "

It was too late. Davinia's voice faded as she observed the frozen expression on the Duke's face. As luck would have it, the sketch which had fallen uppermost from the folder was that of Lord Randal Maunsell.

Davinia had caught Lord Randal as she loved him best, with his head thrown back as if he were on the verge of laughter. There was a teasing, merry expression in his eyes and a warm, tender curve to his full mouth.

The Duke's mouth, as he studied the portrait, was set in a thin line of contempt. Abruptly, he stood up and handed back the sketches to Davinia.

"Strange," he remarked coldly. "Somehow, I would have expected a lady of your temperament to give your heart to a man, not a mere boy. But I see I have misjudged you!"

"How dare you presume to judge, or criticize, or even comment on my character or my choice of companions!" Davinia flared, her green eyes stormy.

The Duke replied curtly, "You are quite correct. I am indeed in error. I had no right to look at that which clearly does not concern me. I beg your pardon. Good afternoon, Miss Davinia."

With that he bowed, turned on his heel, and strode off through the village.

With her head held high, Davinia walked in the other direction, back to Chartcombe Court. She was infuriated to find that her eyes were filled with angry tears. What an insufferable man the Duke was! And what could have been his intention in referring to Lord Randal as a mere boy? Such arrogance!

How dare he presume to interfere in my life, Davinia raged. Each time we meet my loathing for him increases. The sooner he is married to Charlotte the better. No doubt all the other girls in the county will weep a river of tears at his wedding. But I shall be laughing and dancing for joy!

"Excellent sermon this morning," declared Sir William, blinking behind his spectacles as he stepped from the gloom of Bath Abbey into the bright morning sunlight. "Most thought-provoking and uplifting. Do you not agree, Charlotte?"

"Er . . . yes, indeed, Papa. It was extremely interesting." Charlotte, in truth, had not heard a word of the sermon. Throughout the service her eyes had been fixed on the straight back of the Duke of Strathavon, seated four pews in front. With all her heart Charlotte had willed him to turn and observe how fetching she looked in her new green-ribboned bonnet. But to her chagrin, the Duke had remained completely absorbed in his devotions, and had glanced neither to right nor to left.

In view of the settled weather, Sir William suggested that the family take a stroll in the nearby Orange Grove. Lady Lydia, however, noticing that the Duke had not yet emerged from the Abbey, was anxious to remain awhile in its immediate vicinity.

She turned to her niece. "Davinia, dear, I appear to have left my prayer book on the pew. Would you mind fetching it for me? We will wait for you here."

Willingly, Davinia reentered the Abbey. She loved the splendid, soaring lines, the graceful arches and the cool air of tranquility in the ancient building. With the sun shafting through its great windows, the Abbey resembled a magnificent, majestic jewel.

Davinia collected her aunt's prayer book and was making her way back up the aisle when she noticed the Duke of Strathavon standing near the door, deep in conversation with Sir Richard Irwin. Davinia was still smarting from her abrasive encounter with the Duke of yesterday afternoon. She certainly had no desire now to place herself in a situation which would require them both to engage in polite Sunday morning conversation.

Accordingly, she slipped into the shadows of the nave, to allow the Duke time to finish his conversation and leave. Davinia had never ventured before into this part of the Abbey. Her lively curiosity was soon aroused by the tablets of saints and the notable men who had contributed to the glory of the Abbey. Some of the statues were extremely old and crumbly, and Davinia was forced to rely on the brass plaques beneath to determine who they were.

One of the most impressive monuments was to Bishop Montagu. Davinia recalled her uncle telling the charming tale of how the Bishop had walked here one day with the godson of Queen Elizabeth, Sir John Harington.

A downpour of rain had driven them inside the Abbey. But even here they were not protected from the elements, for at that time the nave had no roof. This caused Sir John to remark:

"How, if the church does not save us from water above, shall it save us from fire below?"

The Bishop took the hint, and with the knight's patronage, campaigned for the roofing of the nave. Davinia stood for a while, admiring the workmanship in the sculptured heraldry crowning the pair of columns on the Bishop's monument.

The beautiful statue of St. Peter, too, held her attention for several minutes. The tablet next to St. Peter, however, was chipped and worn, though Davinia could see enough to realize that it represented a fine, strong figure of a man.

Curious to know who he might be, she leaned forward to read the brass plaque:

> King Offa of Mercia, who founded St. Peter's Monastery on this site, in AD 758

Davinia gasped. Taking out her handkerchief, she rubbed it over the brass to make quite sure she had read the inscription correctly. But she had made no mistake.

With trembling fingers, Davinia took from her purse the yellowed piece of parchment Lord Randal had given her. Her eyes fell on the second of the Lady Violetta's clues to the whereabouts of her jewels:

> My second has stood o'er a thousand proud years,
> Since a Mercian King dewed the site with his tears.

124

She *must* mean the Abbey, Davinia reasoned, her eyes sparkling with excitement. Surely there can be no other building in Bath founded over a thousand years ago by a Mercian King?

Glancing round, she saw to her relief that the Duke had now left the Abbey. Davinia hurried outside, hoping to find Lord Randal there. She had noticed him earlier on, seated near the Duke during the service. Now she could not wait to tell him that she had discovered another letter of the riddle.

The Abbey gardens were thronged with the quality of Bath, but to her annoyance Davinia could not see Lord Randal amongst them.

Sir William was calling to her. Davinia was furious to observe that Lady Lydia had succeeded in engaging the Duke of Strathavon in conversation.

He bowed as Davinia approached. "Good morning, Miss Davinia. I trust I find you in excellent health?"

His mocking blue eyes reminded her unmercifully of her undignified scramble to wrest her sketch folder from him.

"I am perfectly well, thank you my lord." She turned to her aunt. "Here is your prayer book, Aunt Lydia."

"Thank you," smiled Lady Lydia. "Such an inspiring service, was it not my lord Duke? We are most honored by your presence here today. I had fear . . . imagined you would perhaps find it more convenient to worship in your own private chapel at Avonley Chantry."

The Duke replied gallantly, "But then I should not have had the pleasure of conversing with you and your family after the service, Lady Lydia."

Charlotte, taking the compliment as solely directed toward herself, simpered coquettishly, and fiddled with the ribbons on her bonnet. Lady Lydia, meanwhile, gave a dry little cough as she quite deliberately dug the point of her parasol into Sir William's foot.

He winced. "Ah . . . yes . . . I, er . . . I wondered, my lord, as we are such immediate neighbors, if you would do us the honor of dining with us at Chartcombe Court one evening?"

The Duke smiled. "I should be delighted, Sir William."

"Would Tuesday suit you, my lord," Lady Lydia pressed. "It will be nothing grand, or formal, mind. Just a small, *family* occasion."

With difficulty, Davinia repressed a smile. So, already, the Duke was being encouraged to consider that the Sinclairs and the Strathavons were as one! Well, that is all to the good, she mused.

The prospect of entertaining the Duke for an entire evening struck Davinia as an appalling ordeal. Nevertheless, she knew it must be borne, and carried off successfully, with Charlotte presented to the best possible advantage.

"Tuesday will suit admirably," replied the Duke. "I shall look forward to it." And with a graceful bow, he took his leave.

Lady Lydia's eyes were shining with triumph. "There, you see, William! I told you he would be civility itself, if only you would just pluck up the courage to ask him!"

"Well, the matter is fixed, and I trust you are perfectly satisfied," murmured Sir William. "Now perhaps we may embark on our stroll round the Orange Grove. Ah, here is Lord Randal Maunsell approaching. Perhaps he would care to join us."

To Davinia's pleasure and delight, Lord Randal declared that a Sunday morning promenade was just the diversion he sought, and, accordingly, the party set off.

"I have never understood," pouted Charlotte, "why this place is called as it is. Why, there is not a single orange in sight!"

Sir William laughed. "It was named in honor of the Prince of Orange, Charlotte. See, over here is an obelisk, erected to celebrate the Prince's recovery from illness after taking the waters at Bath."

As Charlotte and her mother accompanied Sir William to view the obelisk, Davinia seized her chance for a private word with Lord Randal. Swiftly, she told him of her discovery of the statue to King Offa.

"So you see, Lord Randal, the second letter must be *A* for *Abbey!*"

Lord Randal frowned. "Not necessarily, Davinia. Why not *M* for *Monastery*, as that was the original building on this site. Remember, according to the plaque, King Offa founded a monastery, not an abbey."

"But the second letter of the riddle must be a vowel," Davinia insisted. "We know the first is *N*, for Beau *Nash*. But *NM* would not make sense. Yet, *NA* . . ."

"And we already have the sixth letter," said Lord Randal, his face brightening. "*NA − − − V −.*"

"Oh dear," murmured Davinia. "We still have a long way to go."

He pressed her hand. "Take heart. We are making excellent progress, thanks to you. Why, I was convinced I would never be able to unravel any of the clues when first I set eyes on them. Yet, already we know three letters out of the seven."

"You are right," smiled Davinia. "I must learn

to be more patient." But it is so hard when I do so want Lord Randal to find those jewels. For not until then will he feel free to declare his love for me!

"How is the romance progressing between the Duke and Miss Sinclair?" inquired Lord Randal. "I notice he stopped for a word with you all after the service."

"My aunt has invited him to dine with us on Tuesday," said Davinia mournfully. "It is essential to our plans, I know, but I cannot say I view the prospect with any pleasure."

Lord Randal laughed. "My, you have really taken against the Duke! I declare, when you speak of him your eyes glitter as bright as sword blades!"

"I confess, I find him a thoroughly objectionable man," said Davinia vehemently. "The sooner he is married off to Charlotte the better. She is truly welcome to him!"

A cloud had obscured the sun, and Lady Lydia declared, "We must return home, William. The sun has gone in, and I would not wish Charlotte to catch a chill."

Lord Randal said softly to Davinia, "You must join your family. But we shall meet again soon."

He bade farewell to the Sinclairs and then walked jauntily away through the grove. Davinia's eyes followed him until he was out of sight.

Once again she felt a surge of anger as she recalled the Duke's comment about Lord Randal being a mere boy. How dare he! Admittedly, Lord Randal's appearance was youthful, and at twenty-one he could not be expected to possess as much experience in the ways of the world as the Duke. Davinia remembered the Duke as he strode away through the village yesterday afternoon, a confident, imposing figure of a man.

He is just jealous, Davinia decided, because Lord Randal is younger and has more of his life ahead of him. Maturity has clearly soured the Duke. In his middle age, he will become crabby—the sort of man who is forever decrying the vigor of the young.

Yes, that is it. He is merely envious of Lord Randal. And if the Duke presumes to criticize him again, then I shall take great pleasure in informing his lordship that he has fallen prey to a certain infamous green-eyed monster!

"I was given to understand that it is to be an *informal* dinner to which we have invited the Duke," said Sir William peevishly, as he entered the morning room on Monday.

Lady Lydia glanced up from her writing desk, an abstracted expression on her angular face. "I beg your pardon, William? I regret I did not quite catch what you were saying. This dinner menu for tomorrow is causing me so much trouble."

Sir William sighed. "The entire house is in an uproar. The servants are all of a dither. One of the footmen just dropped an entire tray of cleaned silver in the hall. Frightful din. Everywhere I try to walk I tread on maids brushing carpets. And Charlotte's hysterics about her dress can be heard, I have no doubt, by everyone four counties away."

"Why do you not retire to your library?" suggested Lady Lydia soothingly.

"Because," began Sir William with asperity, "Jarvis the Steward informs me that you have given orders for the chimney to be swept, my chairs to be polished with beeswax and all the books taken down and dusted. The room has already been invaded by an army of servants. I'm convinced they won't put the books back in the right places and it will take me months setting it all back as it should be." Sir William sounded thoroughly aggrieved.

"I am sorry you are inconvenienced, William. But I thought it would be a sensible notion for you and the Duke to retire to the library after dinner to enjoy your port and brandy. The dining room is so drafty, you know. I imagine the Duke might find the library more comfortable."

Sir William nodded. "He has expressed a considerable interest in my books. Especially my rare first editions."

"Excellent," smiled Lady Lydia. "But do not tarry too long in the library. It is important that the Duke is given the opportunity of conversing as much as possible with Charlotte." She threw down her quill. "I do hope the dinner will be to his liking."

"Mmm, we do not want indigestion souring his temper and impairing his judgment of Charlotte," murmured Sir William.

Lady Lydia missed the wry note in his voice. "Indeed not, William. Now tell me, do you think this sounds suitable fare? I propose mackerel with green gooseberries, then fillet of veal roasted with truffles—that is Cook's specialty, you know. And to finish, a syllabub, with fresh strawberries and cream."

"That sounds capital," Sir William approved.

Lady Lydia frowned. "But is it your opinion that the Duke will regard it as strange to be served fruit with the first course and the last? And should we perhaps have four courses instead of three? I do not want him to think us mean."

"I am convinced that three courses will do admirably," said Sir William. "And as for the fruit, it seems an excellent notion to serve what is fresh and in season. As a practical man, the Duke will see the sense of that. It is supposed to be a family meal, after all, not a banquet."

Lady Lydia raised a weary hand to her forehead. "I declare, my brow is throbbing. There is so much to do!"

"Can Davinia not assist you?" asked Sir William, dutifully passing his wife her lavender water.

"She is upstairs helping Charlotte decide on her dress for tomorrow night," sighed Lady Lydia. "Now if you will excuse me, William, I must ring for Cook and give her this menu."

"But where am I supposed to go?" demanded Sir William testily. "There does not appear to be a room in the house uninfested with servants, and mops."

"Why not take a refreshing little walk down to your bowling green?" suggested Lady Lydia.

"My dear, it is sheeting with *rain!*" protested Sir William.

"Oh! Is it? Dear me, what a downpour. I have been so absorbed, I did not realize . . . I must remember to tell Jarvis to have some extra gravel laid on the drive. It gets so muddy, you know, after heavy rain, and I would not want the Duke to be splashed on his way here."

"I shall retire to my gun room," declared Sir William, his voice heavy. "And if any servant is so reckless as to set foot in there with a mop, or cleaning rag, I shall blast her silly head off!"

Lady Lydia winced as the door slammed. Really, one could not blame poor William for being so out of temper. Nothing upset him more than being unable to retreat to his beloved library.

But all this confusion is in such a good cause.

Surely he can appreciate that, mused Lady Lydia. This is a golden opportunity to see dear Charlotte married. And married well, too. Such a chance will never come again. It would be foolhardy not to do everything possible to impress the Duke. And when it is all over, and Charlotte is safely departed on her Wedding Tour, I shall insist that William take me away for a well-deserved rest.

Lyme Regis would be pleasant. I have always harbored an affection for Lyme. Though of course with Charlotte's delicate constitution it has been impossible for us to sojourn there for long. The sea air overwhelms her, poor dear.

But when she is safely installed at Avonley Chantry as the Duchess of Strathavon, I shall be free to indulge myself a little more. After all this strenuous activity planning her marriage, I think I deserve a little rest by the sea. And William loves to walk along the cliffs and point out all the different kinds of ships sailing by. Yes, we shall go to Lyme. I must—

There was a knock on the door, and the harrassed cook entered to receive the menu. With a sigh Lady Lydia reluctantly turned her back on the view out to sea, and directed her attention once more to the mackerel.

"You must insure, Cook, that the gooseberries are green, and tart and really fresh . . ."

Upstairs in Charlotte's bedchamber, chaos reigned. Her bed, her sofa, her window seat and her dressing room were strewn with gowns. Davinia and Charlotte's maid, Annie, were limp with exhaustion.

"No, not that sprigged muslin, it makes me look too plump," cried Charlotte, throwing the offending dress onto the pile of others she had discarded.

"Oh, why did Mama choose this Tuesday to invite the Duke? Had she asked him for next week there would have been time for me to have a new dress made."

"Charlotte, the whole purpose of the occasion is to encourage the Duke to feel completely at home with the family. He will hardly feel comfortable if we are all sitting around preening in new dresses," Davinia pointed out.

Charlotte said sharply, "Why do you refer to us *all*, Davinia? There was never any question of *you* having a new gown. It is I, after all, in whom the Duke is interested. It is I who have met and conversed with him on several occasions now. Whereas you are barely acquainted with him, Cousin."

"Indeed, that is so, Charlotte," murmured Davinia, holding up a pale blue dress for Charlotte's approval.

Charlotte shook her head. "No, not the blue mull. It is too thin."

"Then why not the pale pink jackonet," suggested Annie desperately. "Jackonet is heavier muslin than mull."

"But the lace round the neck is not really of the finest quality," complained Charlotte. "I was mortified at the Pump Room recently to notice that Lady Imogen was wearing a dress adorned with lace far superior to mine."

Annie heaped the rejected dresses onto her arms and disappeared into the dressing room. After a few minutes she returned with yet another selection of gowns.

"Now what was I saying to you, Davinia," mused Charlotte. "Oh yes, I recall. About the Duke, and tomorrow's visit. Naturally, you will have to be

133

present, but I hope you will keep yourself as much in the background as possible. You have rather a bold, forward manner, you know, and I have no wish for the Duke to take against me simply because of the unladylike frankness of demeanor of my orphaned cousin."

Fear not, Charlotte, thought Davinia dryly. Your orphaned cousin has no desire to distract the attention of the Duke for even a single minute. I shall sit as still and dumb as a statue. I promise you faithfully, Charlotte, that you shall most certainly be the star of the evening!

Eight

Charlotte spent much of the following day with her hair tied in rags. On her face Annie had smoothed a lotion of elder leaves steeped in wine vinegar, to bleach out a few hated freckles.

Miss Sinclair had decided, at last, on a lilac gown of tamboured muslin, with the embroidered leaf design on the bodice picked out in a double line on the hem. An amethyst necklace and diamond brooch completed her ensemble.

Davinia declared, "You look as pretty as a picture, Charlotte," as the dark-haired girl, with curls triumphantly in place, made her appearance in the drawing room.

Davinia herself had selected, from the limited choice available to her, a dress of plain white muslin, completely unadorned apart from the gold locket around her slender throat. Blessed with a complete lack of vanity, Davinia had no notion how fresh and lovely she looked in her simple gown. Charlotte, by contrast, appeared fussy and over-decorated with her fancy embroidery and glittery jewels.

The Duke arrived punctually, and within the hour they were all seated in the dining room, enjoying the excellent mackerel with green gooseberries.

The Duke inquired if the gooseberries were from Sir William's estate, and on this being confirmed, his lordship commented:

"My gardeners have just started work putting the kitchen garden at Avonley Chantry to rights. There is much to do. Most of the hothouse panes have been smashed and the majority of the soft fruit will have to be replanted. During my late uncle's absence, I regret to say that the estate was often used by the villagers to graze their sheep and goats."

"Outrageous!" murmured Lady Lydia.

"One afternoon, I even caught a local milk-maid lolling in one of my apple trees," said the Duke blandly.

Stung, Davinia could not resist the retort, "If the villagers made free with your land, my lord, your late uncle had only himself to blame for neglecting his duties on the estate."

Charlotte kicked Davinia under the table. Had she not warned her cousin not to dare to presume to address the Duke in such a bold fashion?

The Duke regarded Davinia levelly over the rim of his wine glass, and remarked, "There is some truth in your words, Miss Davinia. However, now I am in residence, I have made it known that I will tolerate no trespassers."

Davinia raised her napkin to conceal her flush. He was deliberately taunting her! And she had foolishly risen to the bait! Well, it shall not happen again, she resolved. For the remainder of the meal, Davinia endeavored to keep her eyes firmly downcast, and would not be drawn into any conversation with the Duke.

When he inquired if she had visited any of the local coastal resorts, she replied primly that she had not had that pleasure, but that Charlotte, last year, had visited her aunt in Lyme Regis.

Charlotte required no further prompting to talk of the delights of her sojourn by the sea.

"But naturally," said Lady Lydia when Charlotte drew breath, "we could not allow her to stay too long. The sea air is just a little *too* bracing for a girl of Charlotte's delicate health. And in truth," Lady Lydia gave a little indulgent laugh, "Charlotte is only really content residing here, in the delightful vicinity of Bath."

Charlotte was on the verge of contesting her mother's remark. She had found Lyme Regis most refreshing. And she had often condemned Bath as a dull place, urging her parents to remove to London.

Now it was Davinia's turn to tap her cousin smartly on the ankle. Catching her aunt's drift, Davinia said helpfully, "I have often heard you sigh, Charlotte, that if you could spend the rest of your days amidst these gentle green hills, then you will be the happiest, most contented girl in the world."

Charlotte hastily swallowed her last spoonful of syllabub. "Oh yes. Quite so. I have no wish to leave this part of Somerset," she gushed, fluttering her lashes appealingly at the Duke.

"The climate here is certainly most temperate," said the Duke. He turned to Sir William. "I believe Admiral Nelson viewed the area with much favor?"

"Yes indeed," nodded Sir William. "He came to Bath, you will mind, to recover from a fever contracted during his West Indian station. He declared that Bath was Bermuda to the rest of England. As a point of fact, I have in the library some of the maps used by Lord Nelson himself. Would you care to see them, my lord?"

"I should be greatly honored," replied the Duke.

Seeing that the menfolk were establishing such an excellent rapport, Lady Lydia hastily gave the signal for the ladies to withdraw.

In the drawing room, Lady Lydia collapsed onto the sofa, and closed her eyes. "My, the strain of this evening is just too, too great," she murmured. "Davinia, would you oblige me by pouring the tea. Though I declare at this moment I feel too overwrought even to raise the cup to my lips."

"The tea will revive you, Aunt," said Davinia, pouring the amber liquid into a delicate Dresden cup. "Tell me, Charlotte, what is your opinion of the Duke now you have had the opportunity to converse with him over dinner?"

Charlotte twisted her handkerchief into a knot. "He is extremely civil," she faltered. "But . . . I confess he still frightens me a little. I do wish he would smile more!"

"He is a *Duke*, not a fawning young dandiprat," said Lady Lydia reprovingly. "He has a title, a vast estate and many responsibilities. It is your task this evening to help him appreciate that you will make a valuable helpmeet as his duchess."

"Yes, Mama," replied Charlotte doubtfully.

Sipping her tea, Davinia reflected that Charlotte was right. The Duke's expression was for the most part grave, and somewhat forbidding. Yet on the rare occasions when he smiled, what a change came over his countenance! Then, Davinia found it impossible to look away from the devastating charm of those brilliant blue eyes.

She choked on her tea. Devastating! Whatever was she dreaming of? To be thinking of this maddening, infuriating, arrogant man in such terms! The wine at dinner must have been stronger than that to which I am accustomed, Davinia decided. Clearly, it is putting absurd fancies into my head.

To concentrate her thoughts, Davinia took up her embroidery and forced herself to tackle a portion which demanded total attention, and the finest of stitches.

The minutes dragged by. An hour passed, but still the gentlemen had not emerged from the library. The three Sinclair ladies lapsed into silence. Each was fully aware that during this hour with the Duke in the library Sir William had promised Lady Lydia to mention the matter of Charlotte's dowry. And, in particular, that she would take with her when she wed the coveted one hundred acres.

How will the Duke react, wondered Davinia, critically examining the neat tracery of stitches at the back of her embroidery. At the very worst, he could decide that a loveless marriage to Charlotte is the last thing he desires. In which case he will make his excuses and be on his way at the soonest opportunity.

But from what Lord Randal had told her, it seemed unlikely that the Duke would act so rashly. He had never, according to Lord Randal, been in love in his life. Which was not at all surprising,

139

Davinia considered, when one examined his temperament. And on the opposite side of the coin, which woman in the world would be so foolish as to give her heart to a man as arrogant as he?

No, the level-headed Duke was seeking a marriage of convenience. And who could be more convenient than Charlotte, his neighbor's daughter, and with the promise of the one hundred acres in her dowry?

At last the drawing room doors opened to admit the men. The Duke's countenance was, as always, infuriatingly unreadable. But from the faint smile playing around Sir William's lips, Davinia judged that he was far from displeased with his discussion with the Duke.

Lady Lydia rang for fresh tea to be served, and inquired of the Duke how work was progressing at Avonley Chantry.

"All is well under control now, I am pleased to say, Lady Lydia," said the Duke in his deep, well-modulated voice. "My new baliff seems a responsible fellow, and I am confident that the carpenters and decorators will have completed their work in another month. My immediate concern, however, is the cleaning of the portraits. In fact, I shall be in Bath tomorrow morning to see how my picture restorer is progressing with the work."

Sir William said, "I hear the portraits are some of the finest in all southern England?"

"They are indeed, and I feel it is my cultural duty to ensure that they are displayed to their best advantage." The Duke spread his hands in a disarming gesture. "I only wish I could paint myself. But to my regret I am quite ungifted in that direction. It occurs to me that living in this glorious countryside must provide endless inspiration to any-one blessed with artistic talent."

Davinia caught his mocking eyes upon her. This time, she thought grimly, I shall refuse to rise to his bait. I shall not take his remarks personally, as he clearly intends me to.

She remarked, in a polite, social tone, "Of course, Mr. Gainsborough accomplished some of his finest work in Bath. Do you have any of his paintings at Avonley Chantry, my lord?"

Davinia was quite well aware, from her own wanderings around his house, that the Duke owned not a single Gainsborough.

"I am not particularly impressed with Mr. Thomas Gainsborough," declared the Duke dismissively. "I favor Sir Joshua Reynolds' style."

Davinia raised a surprised eyebrow. "But Mr. Gainsborough's portraits exhibit such depth of *feeling*."

"Sir Joshua, Miss Davinia, was a painter of *intellect*."

"Yet he could never capture Mr. Gainsborough's delicate effects of light."

The Duke's mouth tightened. "Sir Joshua was more concerned—nay, was the master—of substance and pose."

"But Mr. Gainsborough was such a fine drafts-man. And the light, creamy texture of his paint knows no equal."

"Certainly, I would agree that he appeals to the feminine mind," said the Duke scornfully.

"I do not profess to understand a thing about Mr. Gainsborough's art," hurriedly interposed Sir William, "but I do recall that during the sixteen years he lived in Bath, Mr. Gainsborough increased his prices from five to an outrageous one hundred guineas. Then, of course, he had a vicious quarrel with one of the local dignitaries and never set foot in Bath again."

"That appears to have been quite a fashionable course of action in distinguished circles," murmured Davinia serenely, handing the Duke his tea.

Her subtlety was not lost on him. For an instant his eyes flashed. He had grasped her reference to his uncle's quarrel with Sir William over the price of the hundred acres. The old Duke, like Thomas Gainsborough, had departed in a huff for London, never to return.

But would the Duke remember her prediction as Madame Dresson, when she had foretold the ending of a feud, and the signing of a treaty which would possibly be linked with a dowry. Had she, in fact, managed to convince him that it was his rightful destiny to marry Charlotte?

Lady Lydia rattled her teacup, clearly displeased that her daughter had been for so long excluded from the conversation.

"Charlotte, I am convinced you are sitting in a draft. Would you like me to have a screen sent in?" She smiled at the Duke. "Charlotte is so precious to us. She has such a delicate, fragile constitution. Why, I will not even allow her to travel in an open carriage, for fear of her catching a chill."

Horrified, Davinia watched Lady Lydia reach out to pull the bell, and summon a footman with the screen.

"Oh, my dearest Aunt, I was hoping you would ask Charlotte to play for us on the pianoforte," said Davinia quickly.

The last thing she desired was for the Duke to regard Charlotte as a sickly, weak creature. The

Duke required a robust, healthy girl as his duchess. A whey-faced invalid bride would be nothing but a burden, threatening to interfere with his plans to spend most of his married life in London, and alone.

Davinia continued persuasively, "Charlotte plays quite divinely, my lord. Sir William, will you not prevail upon Charlotte to entertain us?"

Sir William, with fatherly pride, urged his daughter toward the instrument. Davinia breathed a sigh of relief that the dangerous topic of drafts, chills and ailing daughters was forgotten.

Contentedly, she settled back to listen to Charlotte, happy for her cousin to be the center of attraction. Yet for the remainder of the evening, she was uncomfortably aware that the Duke's gaze rested more often on her than on the girl he should be contemplating making his bride.

"In view of the weather," announced Lady Lydia as the rain lashed against the breakfast parlor windows, "I am of the opinion that it would be prudent to postpone our visit to Bath."

"But Mama, we *must* go!" wailed Charlotte. "The Duke remarked that he would be in Bath himself this morning. It would be foolish to pass up the opportunity of a chance meeting."

Lady Lydia frowned. "Really, Charlotte, you must not be observed chasing the Duke hither and thither all over Bath. It is too vulgar. Altogether too *fast*."

Davinia hurried to her cousin's support. She, also, was anxious to make the short journey into Bath, but not to see the Duke. It was Lord Randal Maunsell whom Davinia hoped to encounter.

"My dear Aunt, permit me to assure you that

143

no one could ever entertain the notion of Charlotte being in any way forward. Why, her manners toward the Duke have been the very soul of propriety. And I do believe I can detect a break in the clouds over the hills. I am convinced the rain will stop soon."

Davinia was proved right. By half past ten there was sufficient blue sky for Lady Lydia to order the carriage. She herself was secretly only too pleased to be making one of her rare excursions out of Chartcombe Court, as she hoped to meet Lady Selina at the Pump Room. Partly, of course, to glory in having persuaded the Duke to dine with them last night. But also because she desired a sympathetic married woman's ear over her latest domestic problem.

Even in the crowded Pump Room, Lady Selina's vivid puce muslin was instantly visible. Lady Lydia hurried forward to greet her, and was soon pouring out her complaints about her new laundry maid who had, as she put it, "fallen from grace."

"It really is so vexing," sighed Lady Lydia. "I know if my Mama were still alive she would be shocked to hear me discussing backstairs activities. But I declare, Lady Selina, one cannot turn a blind eye to these matters forever. This is the third girl to become *enceinte* in the past year. I cannot imagine what it is about laundry maids which renders them so susceptible to unsuitable male charms."

"I have the same trouble myself," said Lady Selina. "But I do not see what one can do about it. After all, what with all the steam, and that disagreeable soapy odor coming from the laundry, it is essential to site it at an extremity of the house.

144

And it has to be near a large area of open drying ground. So, inevitably, one finds that the only suitable place for the laundry is near the stables . . ."

"And stableboys being what they are, the result is ruined laundry maids," murmured Lady Lydia. "I think in future I shall ensure that all my laundry staff are securely married before they are employed." As the orchestra struck up a merry tune, she went on, "Fortunately, Cook seems a great deal more settled now, so my worries have abated on that score. By the by, we enjoyed such a pleasant evening yesterday. The Duke of Strathavon came to dine with us."

Lady Selina's eyebrows rose. "Oh! You were indeed honored. He has been accepting so few social engagements, as supervising the renovation of his house is taking so much of his time. Lady Irwin, I understand, was most huffed when he declined her dinner invitation."

"Strictly *entre nous*" whispered Lady Lydia, raising her fan, "the Duke is quite taken with Charlotte. It warms my heart to see how well they look together. But naturally, Lady Selina, Charlotte is such a tender little flower, she would be most distressed if it were common knowledge in society that the Duke is so attached to her."

"You may rely on me, I shall not breathe a word," promised a wide-eyed Lady Selina.

Lady Lydia smiled, confident that by this time tomorrow morning Lady Selina would have ensured that all Bath had heard the news.

Charlotte, disappointed that the Duke was not taking the waters in the Pump Room, suggested to Davinia that they partake of a stroll. After the rain, the pavements were quickly drying out in the warm sun to their distinctive pale honey shade.

Charlotte's sharp brown eyes were everywhere as she searched for the Duke. Davinia's private opinion was that Charlotte would never find the Duke of Strathavon aimlessly promenading the fashionable streets of Bath. That, he would consider a complete waste of his time. No, once his business here was concluded, Davinia could well imagine him ensconced in one of the city's excellent libraries —Duffield's, perhaps, in Milsom Street—absorbing himself in the latest newspapers and magazines from England and France.

As they turned into Bond Street, Charlotte was soon diverted by attempting display of bonnets in the milliner's window.

"Oh, see, Davinia, such adorable coquelicot ribbons on that straw! And isn't that ruched satin style divine? I do so love pretty things. But if I order any more bonnets Papa would be sure to fling the house from the windows. He declares that from the milliner's bills he receives I must already have enough bonnets and caps to wear a different one every day of the year."

"Console yourself with the thought," smiled Davinia, "that when you are the Duchess of Strathavon you will be free to indulge your whims as much as you wish."

"It is a pleasant prospect," agreed Charlotte gravely. "I shall wear the very latest modes, and there will be balls, and concerts, oh, every kind of entertainment at Avonley Chantry. And yet," she continued wistfully, "I fear I shall be lonely."

"Why so?" asked Davinia.

"Because if the Duke does marry me, it will not be for love," declared Charlotte. "I suspect that he will leave me here in Bath, and spend most of his time in London. He will not desire me to ac-

146

company him. And how I should love to reside in London! I find Bath society so slow, so dull!"

Here Davinia could not agree. She adored the easy, agreeable pace of this friendly city. After crowded, bustling, jostling London, Davinia appreciated the wide crescent, the graceful terraces and spacious streets of Bath. She felt at home, here, in this elegant city set in the beautiful valley of green hills.

She was, however, a little disturbed at Charlotte's unexpected insight into the conditions of a marriage with the Duke. Davinia had not realized that Charlotte was so perceptive, and she could not help but feel sympathy for her cousin. True, if Charlotte married the Duke she would be the envied mistress of a beautiful country house, and the leader of Somerset society.

Yet her husband, as Charlotte rightly surmised, would be absent for much of the year. And there would be no passion, no wild ecstasy in Charlotte's life. For hers would be a loveless marriage.

Yet, in truth, who could possibly tell in advance how one would fare if wedded to the Duke? Although his name had never been seriously linked with any woman, it was no secret that he had enjoyed many affairs. He was an experienced man of the world.

How, then, would he approach his trembling bride? With kindness and a gentle concern, courting her with courtesy and infinite tenderness? Or would he storm into her bedchamber, take her into his arms, and tearing her nightgown asunder, cover her face, her throat, her bosom with brutal, savage kisses . . .

"Davinia! You nearly stepped right into the path of that sedan! What *are* you dreaming of?"

147

Davinia blushed to the roots of her golden hair. What had she been dreaming of indeed! Whatever ails you, Davinia, she silently reproached herself. Allowing your thoughts to wander in such a wanton fashion! Are you deranged?

Hastily, Davinia put up her parasol, fearing that the sun was bringing on a fever. Fortunately, before she had time to reflect further on the matter, Charlotte spied Lord Randal Maunsell. He was bowling down the street in fine style in a handsome gig, drawn by a spirited, high-stepping gray.

"Good morning, ladies!" he called. "What is your opinion of my new gig? Is it not just the style?"

"It is certainly most impressive," agreed Davinia. And dreadfully expensive, she reflected, wondering anxiously where the financially distressed Lord Randal had found the funds for such a vehicle.

"I took possession this morning, and couldn't wait to go for a spin," grinned the young man. "Wait! I have a capital notion! You two ladies must join me for a short ride around the town."

Charlotte shook her head and said primly, "I regret, I am not permitted to travel in open carriages, my lord."

There was not, in any event, room for both ladies to travel in comfort in the gig.

Lord Randal did not attempt to persuade her. "So you are intent on depriving me of your charming company, Miss Sinclair. Well, so be it. But I hope I will have the pleasure of seeing you at the Summer Ball at the Assembly Rooms?"

"When is that?" inquired Davinia.

"A week on Thursday," he replied. "I am aware that Lady Lydia is not often persuaded to attend the Assembly Rooms. But this is to be a special occasion. *Everyone*," he said meaningfully, "will be there."

"Then so shall we," declared Charlotte decisively. "I shall speak to Mama at the first opportunity." She turned to Davinia. "Now you must not allow me to spoil your pleasure, Davinia. *You* must go for a ride with Lord Randal."

"But I cannot leave you here alone," protested Davinia.

Charlotte looked evasive. "I . . . I have just observed Lady Imogen in the pastry shop. I shall be delighted to pass the time of day with her for a while."

"That's fixed then," smiled Lord Randal. "We shall be no more than half an hour, Miss Sinclair."

"I shall be perfectly safe and well occupied until then," nodded Charlotte. "Though you must take care not to go too fast, Lord Randal."

Davinia allowed Lord Randal to assist her into the gig, though not without grave misgivings. Charlotte was behaving most strangely. Apart from that sly expression on her face, it was quite out of character for Charlotte to behave charitably toward her cousin. Especially to the extent of wishing her well on a ride with Lord Randal.

However, Davinia was given no opportunity to change her mind. No sooner was she seated than the gray set off at a cracking pace toward Queen's Square.

Lord Randal's exhilarated expression revealed his delight in his new toy.

"Isn't she a dream! Just see how we bowl along!"

"It is indeed an admirable gig," said Davinia breathlessly, "Though workmanship of this excellence does not, I believe, come cheap."

He took her hint. "Ah. I must confess Sir

Richard Irwin was good enough to advance me a sum that would satisfy the coachbuilder. 'Fraid my credit is not too good in this town at present. Damn man insisted on cash in his hand before he'd allow me to take the gig from his yard. Sir Richard lent me the gray, too. Spirited little thing, isn't she?"

Davinia was unable to conceal her distress. "My lord, I understood you were heavily in debt to your cousin, the Duke of Strathavon. Is it really wise to add to your financial burdens by accepting a loan from Sir Richard?"

Lord Randal's laugh rang out as he directed the gig up Gay Street. "But this is only a temporary financial difficulty in which I find myself. Why, when we discover the whereabouts of Violetta's jewels, then all our problems will vanish into the clear blue sky!"

Davinia found it impossible to share his light-hearted attitude. How best could she advise him, in the most tactful manner, to exercise more caution?

She was absorbed in phrasing a few diplomatic words on this theme, when Lord Randal suddenly brought the gig to a halt.

"Davinia!" he cried. "Where are we?"

She glanced round in surprise. They were encircled by elegant houses, each fronted by iron railings. "Why, this is the Circus, of course."

Lord Randal gazed at her intently. "Precisely! Do you not remember:

Round my fifth horses trot—not common or low,
'Tis elegant here—not a travelling show!

Davinia gasped. "Oh, Lord Randal, how brilliant of you! The *Circus*. Admittedly, it is not one of your Aunt Violetta's better couplets. But it serves its purpose. And no doubt in her time, too, all the young bucks came here as they do today to show their new mounts."

He nodded. "It suddenly struck me as we were circling round. So that makes the fifth letter a *C*, for *Circus*. Now what does that give us? We have *N* for *Nash*, *A* for the *Abbey*, then two blanks and a *C* and a *V* . . ."

"*NA – – CV – ?*" said Davinia, doubtfully. "That cannot be correct."

Lord Randal tapped his whip impatiently against the side of the gig. "No, it doesn't make sense. Perhaps Violetta was referring to the shape of the Circus. *R* for *Ring?* No, that's even worse: *NA – – RV –*. Oh, confound the woman! Why did she have to make her clues so dashed difficult?"

"Wait!" Davinia's eyes were sparkling. "You are right about the shape of the Circus. It is a *circle*. And a circle written down—"

"*NA – – OV – !*" cried Lord Randal. "Why, that has a much sounder ring to it!" He laughed at his joke. "Davinia, you are the most clever, the most wonderful, the most beautiful girl in the world!"

Exuberantly, he clasped her to him and planted a smacking kiss on her cheek.

"Lord Randal!" she laughed, struggling in vain to disengage herself. "This is a public place!"

"What could be more fitting? For I want the entire world to know how much I adore you," he smiled, with his arms still around her and in his eyes that teasing, tender expression she loved so much.

At that moment the gray moved forward a few paces, disturbed by the furious speed of a rider galloping past. Lord Randal hastily tightened his hold on the reins, controlling his horse. But Davinia sat immobile in the gig, the laughter frozen to horror on her lovely face.

For the man who had ridden past at such a frightening pace had been none other than the Duke of Strathavon. And fast though he was traveling, she had nevertheless caught his expression of scorn and contempt as he witnessed Lord Randal embracing her.

Davinia's throat felt dry. "We must go back," she said faintly. "Charlotte will be wondering what has become of me."

Lord Randal had not realized that they had been observed by the Duke of Strathavon. "What a capital day this has been, Davinia! I own a new gig, I have you sitting beside me, and we have discovered another letter to lead us to the jewels! I declare, I am the most fortunate man in all England"

He set Davinia down in Bond Street, and before he left he engaged her for the first two dances at the forthcoming Summer Ball. Normally, Davinia would have been dazed with delight at such a happy outcome of her chance meeting with Lord Randal. But seeing the Duke of Strathavon, and in such embarrassing circumstances, had strangely unsettled her. Despite the warmth of the sun she felt chilled, while inside her white gloves her hands were shaking.

There was no sign of Charlotte in the pastry shop, or in any other of the establishments in Bond Street. Davinia decided that her cousin must have grown tired of waiting, and made her way back to the Pump Room.

Lady Lydia and Lady Selina were seated near the statue of Beau Nash, drinking glasses of mineral water. Nearby, Lady Selina's plump daughter, Imogen, was leafing through the social pages of the latest London magazines.

"Is Charlotte not with you?" Davinia asked Lady Imogen in some alarm. "I understood she was to join you in the pastry shop in Bond Street?"

Lady Imogen gazed at her in hurt surprise. "How can you be so cruel as to mention the word *pastry!* You know Mama will not allow me to go within a hundred paces of that shop." She sighed. "I declare, I eat less and less every day, yet still my dresses remain uncomfortably tight round the waist. How do you keep your figure so beautifully neat, Davinia? Please tell me your secret?"

Davinia shook her head. "At this moment I am losing pounds just worrying where Charlotte might be."

Lady Lydia caught Davinia's last words. "You mean you have lost Charlotte?" she cried accusingly.

"Not *lost,* Aunt. I went for a short ride with Lord Randal in his new gig, and when I returned to Bond Street, Charlotte had unaccountably disappeared."

Lady Lydia seemed ready to swoon. Before she could do so, however, Lady Selina said briskly:

"There is no cause for alarm, Lady Lydia. See, there is Charlotte now, just entering the room."

Charlotte is looking extremely pleased with herself, thought Davinia. I wonder what mischief she has been up to?

"Now where have you been, Charlotte?" demanded Lady Lydia. "I have been desperately worried!"

"I walked up to visit my modiste," replied Charlotte smugly. "You see, Mama, Lord Randal informed me that there is to be a Summer Ball at the Assembly Rooms and—"

"Charlotte, you know I cannot abide these Assembly Room dances," said Lady Lydia dismissively. "I fainted three times at the last one. The crush was unbearable."

"Lord Randal did mention, Aunt, that *everyone* in society will be there," murmured Davinia.

There was a short silence. "I see," intoned Lady Lydia reflectively. "Indeed? Well, in that event, of course we shall all attend."

"I went to see the modiste, to order a new gown for the ball," Charlotte informed them breathlessly. "She showed me the most exquisite new muslin, embroidered with flowers and leaves, in the most delicate pinks, blues, yellows and greens, with the leaves and stalks picked out in silver gilt thread!"

As Charlotte spoke she darted a triumphant look at Lady Imogen. She too patronized the same dressmaker and would be furious that Charlotte had been so quick off the mark in securing the most exclusive material for her gown.

A frown creased Lady Lydia's brow. "But, Charlotte, the modiste lives right at the top of Lansdown Street. Surely you did not walk all the way up that hill?"

"Yes, Mama."

Lady Lydia rounded on Davinia. "Really, Niece, this is too bad of you! I am extremely displeased. It seems I cannot leave you for a minute but that you are betraying my trust in you. Whatever possessed you, leaving poor little Charlotte all on her own, and allowing her to tax her delicate strength on a fatiguing walk up that steep hill! We must return home directly. And you shall rest for the remainder of the day, Charlotte."

Davinia glanced at her cousin, waiting for Charlotte to explain that she had urged Davinia to accompany Lord Randal . . . that Charlotte had insisted she would be safely occupied in the pastry shop.

But Charlotte stood with her brown eyes downcast and her thin mouth firmly closed.

The ride back to Chartcombe Court was not enjoyable for Davinia. For much of the journey Lady Lydia chastised Davinia for her thoughtless, irresponsible behavior toward her cousin. Finally, Charlotte, clearly suffering from a guilty conscience, diverted her mother's attention by chattering cheerfully about the Summer Ball. And the possibility— nay, certainty—of the Duke's attending.

Davinia stared with unseeing eyes at the view from the carriage window. What a strangely unsettling morning it had been! On the one hand, she had been delighted to meet Lord Randal and to discover with him the fourth letter of the riddle.

But how she squirmed at the memory of the Duke's face as he galloped by. Oh, what scorn and contempt had been written there! Why, oh why, had he chosen to ride past at that particular moment, just when Lord Randal was embracing me?

And why, a perplexed Davinia asked herself, should the Duke's opinion matter so much to me?

Nine

"Now where is your father?" Lady Lydia demanded, as Charlotte entered the drawing room, dressed for the Summer Ball. "The dancing starts at six o'clock prompt and I am most anxious that we should be there for the beginning. Don't tell me that William has forgotten all about the Ball?"

A footman was dispatched to fetch Sir William. He emerged, looking a trifle dazed, from his library, whence he had retired an hour previous, having grown weary of waiting for the ladies to complete their toilettes.

"I thought you were never going to be ready," he complained mildly. "So I just sat down for five minutes with a book. And suddenly, a whole hour had slipped by."

He smiled his thanks as Davinia thoughtfully

brushed a few specks of snuff from the lapel of his evening coat.

"Do I look well, Papa?" pirouetted Charlotte. "Do you like my new dress?"

"I think you all look quite exquisite," replied Sir William diplomatically.

Indeed, the Sinclair ladies did present a charming picture, with Charlotte in her new embroidered dress and Lady Lydia gowned in forget-me-not blue. Davinia, having very little choice of dresses, was wearing her plain white muslin, onto the hem of which she had sewn a length of heavy gold fringing. Apart from a small gold brooch, her only adornment was the white and gold ribbon which held her silken ringlets in place. Her appearance was one of elegant simplicity, enlivened by the sparkle of excitement in her lovely green eyes.

Sir William pulled the bell, and requested the carriage to be brought round.

"I am still amazed, Lydia," he said, "that you wish to attend the Assembly Ball at all. You know you always complain so of the crush. And I recall you were most upset last time when Sir Richard Irwin whirled you round so fast in the country dancing that the hem of your dress ripped on a loose board."

"There are times in life," Lady Lydia informed him archly, "when one must sacrifice one's own feelings for the future happiness of one's daughter. The Duke of Strathavon will be present this evening, and I am most anxious that everyone should witness the favorable attention he is certain to pay to Charlotte."

Charlotte nervously twisted the fingers of her gloves. "He *will* engage me for a dance, won't he, Mama?"

"If he does not, then we may consider our hopes quite dashed," confessed Lady Lydia. "William, you did mention to the Duke the matter of the hundred acres, and Charlotte's dowry?"

"Of course. As you know, I introduced the subject over our port and brandy in the library when he came to dine with us. The Duke listened most attentively. But he possesses the sort of countenance, you know, which leaves one quite unable to fathom what he is really thinking."

Jarvis was at the door. "The carriage awaits, Sir William."

The carriage set the Sinclair party down at the Bennet Street entrance to the Upper Assembly Rooms. Lady Lydia hurried Charlotte through the business of depositing their cloaks in the lobby, and then swept her through into the ballroom, where the dancing was shortly to commence.

"Quickly now, Charlotte," urged Lady Lydia. "I just noticed Lady Belsover entering the ballroom with her two daughters. It will be too mortifying if the Duke engages them for dances before you."

Davinia was delayed by a distressed Lady Imogen. "Davinia, please give me your truthful opinion. Does this dress make me look fubsy? I could not ask Charlotte, as she would be bound to give me an unkind answer, just to tease. I know you will be honest."

Lady Imogen's dress was of fine gray, silver and blue stripes. Privately, Davinia considered the colors a little ageing on one who was not yet twenty, but she smiled reassuringly and replied, "No indeed, Lady Imogen, the downward stripes lend height to your figure. You do not look at all overweight. The dress is quite delightful, truly."

Lady Imogen's face brightened, and together

159

the two girls made their entrance into the ballroom. It had been charmingly decorated for the Summer Ball with banks of sweet-scented pink roses and twists of honeysuckle.

"Oh!" exclaimed Lady Imogen in amazement. "Just look, Davinia!"

Davinia followed her gaze and observed that the Duke of Strathavon was leading Charlotte onto the floor for the first dance. Lady Lydia, seated on one of the side benches, was wreathed in smiles.

As she watched the pair—the tall commanding figure of the Duke and the frail, white-faced Charlotte—Davinia experienced the stab of an emotion she could not immediately identify. Seeing them standing side by side, waiting for the music to begin, she felt chillingly disturbed. Though for the life of her, Davinia could not imagine why.

A hand touched her arm. "Ah, there you are Davinia! How enchanting you look. I am come to claim the first of my two dances with you."

She gazed up into the laughing, handsome face of Lord Randal Maunsell. With what pleasure she accompanied him onto the floor for the cotillion!

As the dance progressed, Davinia felt her eyes drawn toward the Duke. His grave expression seemed at odds with the gaiety of the occasion. Yet she had to admit he moved superbly, with a natural dignity and grace. Charlotte, beside him, appeared nervous, and missed her step on several occasions. But the Duke's hand was always there to steady her, and Davinia noticed him murmur a few words to his partner which brought a smile to her wan lips.

Once, as Davinia's set passed the Duke's, their eyes met. Conscious of his gaze upon her, Davinia threw back her head and made a soft, laughing remark to Lord Randal. See, she signaled to the Duke, what a fine pair Lord Randal and I make! Your sour, jealous words about him have no effect on me. Oh, how we are enjoying ourselves!

At the end of her two dances with Lord Randal, Davinia returned to sit with her aunt. Lady Lydia's eyes were still fixed on her daughter, who had been escorted by the Duke to join Sir William, on the opposite side of the ballroom.

"Well," sighed Lady Selina, "he has certainly singled Charlotte out this evening, Lady Lydia. All Bath will be buzzing with it in the Pump Room tomorrow."

"I assure you, it is quite a settled thing," smiled Lady Lydia happily. "It is just a matter of time before he formally approaches William to ask for her hand. Don't they make a perfectly matched couple!"

Lady Imogen remarked sulkily, "I am surprised that Charlotte looks with such favor on the Duke. I should never desire to marry such a frightening man."

"There is nothing terrifying, Imogen, about an income of over 50,000 pounds a year," said Lady Lydia briskly.

Abruptly, Lady Imogen stood up. "Oh! The Duke himself is approaching!" she stammered. "If he asked me to dance I should faint with apprehension. Excuse me!"

She hurried away to the shelter and safety of the supper room. Davinia was puzzled.

Whatever ails these girls—both Charlotte and Lady Imogen—that they persist in feeling frightened of the Duke? He is arrogant and overbearing, to be sure. But I would die rather than admit that I was terrified of him!

He bowed to the three ladies. Then to her surprise, Davinia realized he was addressing her.

"Miss Davinia, will you give me the pleasure of partnering you in the minuet?"

Seared in Davinia's memory was his contemptuous look when he galloped past Lord Randal's gig in the Circus. She heard herself reply:

"I am honored by your request, my lord, but I regret that I have no desire to dance again this evening."

She stood up, curtsyed politely, and leaving a stunned silence behind her, walked with head held high to join Sir William.

Tit for tat, my lord Duke, thought Davinia, her lustrous eyes glittering defiantly. *That* will teach you to curl your lip at me in such a scornful fashion!

All the girls in the Assembly Rooms, it appears, are either falling over themselves for your attention, or are too frightened even to look at you. But I, you see, am made of different metal. I am completely indifferent to you. I, alone, of every woman here, can refuse you a dance, turn my back, and walk right away from you, without giving the matter another thought.

Nevertheless, Davinia found herself strangely close to tears. Her throat felt tight, and her eyelids were beginning to sting in the most telltale fashion.

"Hello, my dear. You look a trifle flushed," remarked Sir William kindly. "Are you quite well?"

Davinia smiled ruefully. "I have just refused to dance with the Duke of Strathavon. But of course I now realize that having done that, I am forbidden to set foot on the dance floor for the rest of the evening. And I do so love to dance!"

It is that, reasoned Davinia, which is making me

feel so upset. Oh, curse the Duke! My wretched feud with him has ruined what promised to be a most enjoyable evening. It is all his fault, she decided angrily. If he had behaved more reasonably toward me, and not presumed to pass critical judgment on my friendship with Lord Randal, then none of this would have occurred.

Sir William was watching Sir Richard Irwin partnering Charlotte in the minuet. "I have always thought it odd," he commented, "that such a pleasurable activity like the dance should be hedged around with so many rules of etiquette. It certainly seems unreasonably harsh to me that if you choose not to stand with one gentleman, then you must remain a mere observer for the rest of the evening. Still," he sighed, "you should count yourself lucky you are not living a hundred years ago. In those days, young ladies often had the most miserable time at the Assembly Balls presided over by Mr. Nash."

"Do you refer to the time when he was Master of Ceremonies in Bath?" asked Davinia, grateful for a conversational diversion to take her mind from her own troubles.

Sir William nodded. "Oh yes, protocol was very strict. Mr. Nash would approach the gentleman of highest rank and invite him to dance with the most superior lady present. After two minutes, another gentleman would be encouraged to engage another lady for a dance. Only one couple was allowed on the floor at any given time, so the poor girl was the cynosure of all eyes."

"How terrible if she put a foot wrong!" exclaimed Davinia.

"Disaster," agreed Sir William. "And in those days, the minuet was performed in very slow measure, with great dignity. The ebullient style of someone like Sir Richard Irwin would most certainly have been frowned upon."

He paused for a moment to consider the exuberant Sir Richard treading for the sixth time on Charlotte's foot in the minuet.

"Even smiling," Sir William continued, "was considered most unbecoming. My mother often told me how young girls shivered with fear as they were led out to dance. In truth, she herself was frequently in such a quake, she would hide at the furthest corner of the Lower Rooms until eight o'clock struck and Mr. Nash gave the signal for the country dancing to begin. Then, with the ordeal of the solo minuets over, everyone could relax and begin to enjoy themselves."

The word *ordeal* had struck a chord within Davinia. "Sir William, did you say these dances took place at the Lower Rooms?"

He smiled, heartened by her interest. His dear Charlotte was an adorable girl, of course, but it was quite impossible to converse with her on any but the most trivial level. Yet here was his pretty young niece, Davinia, listening with rapt attention to his every word.

"At that time, Davinia, the building down near the Orange Grove was the only Assembly Room in Bath, and all the balls were held there. Then when the present excellent Assembly Rooms in which we now stand were opened in, I believe 1771, they became known as the Upper Rooms, whilst those down at the Orange Grove were termed the Lower."

Davinia was hardly able to contain her excitement. After a respectable interval, she excused herself and searched amongst the crowded ballroom for Lord Randal. For if his Aunt Violetta had been writing her riddle clues after 1771, then Davinia was positive she had found the answer to the fourth couplet:

To the shadows of four many ladies would steal,
For to dance but a step was a blushing ordeal.

The Lower Rooms! *NA – LOV –* ! Now there was progress. Admittedly, the word still did not make sense. But with only two more letters to find, surely the jewels were almost within Lord Randal's grasp.

But where was Lord Randal? After twenty minutes, inching her way through the thronged ballroom, Davinia was convinced he was not there. Then her instinct told her to look in the Card Room. Sure enough, she found him seated at one of the baize-covered card tables, absorbed in a game of piquet with the portly Lord Alston.

Lord Randal glanced up in some irritation as Davinia's shadow fell across the table. "Davinia, I cannot talk now. I am at a very crucial stage in the game."

"Just answer me one question," said Davinia urgently. "Do you happen to know when Violetta wrote those clues? Which year?"

Lord Randal sighed. "Dash it all, Davinia! How can I be expected to remember a detail like that?"

"Well, when was she married?" asked Davinia desperately.

"My dear, I am trying to play piquet! I have a hundred guineas at stake here!"

"Think!" pleaded Davinia. "It is most important. The answer could lead you to a thousand times a hundred guineas!"

His blue eyes widened in understanding. "I say, Davinia. Do you mean you are on the track of—"

"Yes." Davinia glanced warningly at Lord Alston who was listening with growing interest to the conversation.

"Excuse me just one moment, Lord Alston. This is indeed a matter of vital importance." Lord Randal closed his eyes, one long finger tapping his forehead. "I have seen their marriage date written someplace. Now where? Within my house in Bath . . . ah! I have it! There is a portrait of Violetta and her husband, painted just after their return from their Wedding Tour. I was looking at it just the other day. And yes, I am sure I am correct, the artist had put the date after his initials in the right-hand corner. It says 1770."

Davinia clasped her hands in triumph. "So they would have reached their . . . financial crisis a few years later? I am right then!"

She seized one of the cards, and unpinning the gold brooch from her dress, she scratched on it: *NA – LOV – .*

"There!" she exclaimed, showing Lord Randal the card. "We have only two more letters to find."

"I say, Miss Davinia, you have marked the card!" protested Lord Alston. "The game is ruined. And I was set to win!"

"Hang it, Alston. I dispute that!" glared Lord Randal.

"Oh, I do beg your pardon!" smiled Davinia artlessly. "But you can always call for another pack."

"There is no time," grumbled Lord Alston. "I must leave directly. I am quitting Bath tomorrow for my wedding in Yorkshire, and I have much still to arrange."

"A thousand apologies," murmured Davinia, thankful that she had at least saved Lord Randal the loss of a hundred precious guineas.

As the aggrieved Lord Alston departed, Lord Randal wagged his finger at Davinia. "You are a naughty girl! In my opinion, all young ladies should be taught from the cradle never to come between a gentleman and his cards."

"There!" exclaimed Davinia. "And I had imagined you would be pleased with me for solving another part of the riddle. However, if you are not interested in hearing how I came to realize that the fourth letter was *L*, then I shall return to the ballroom . . . "

He seized her arm. "No, no. I spoke only in jest. Of course I wish to hear."

When Davinia had finished her account Lord Randal was smiling in amazement. "What a splendidly knowledgable gentleman your uncle is! I declare, there is not a subject under the sun about which he does not know at least one fascinating fact."

"At least it proves Aunt Lydia wrong," laughed Davinia. "She is convinced that during most of the hours Sir William spends closeted in his library, he is in truth contentedly snoozing, instead of poring over one musty tome or another."

"*NA – LOV – ,*" mused Lord Randal, a frown etched on his brow. "It is proving to be an uncommonly strange word. The form of it is quite unrecognizable to me."

"And to me," agreed Davinia. "But my instinct says that if we can only solve one more clue, and find one more letter, then all will be revealed. I am convinced of it."

"Then we must place our faith in your feminine instinct," smiled Lord Randal, taking her hands in his. "Now come, we are here to dance, are we not? And the musicians have just struck up Strip the

Willow. It is one of my favorites. Let us hurry to the ballroom and join a set."

"Oh, I regret I cannot parner you, Lord Randal," faltered Davinia. "You see, earlier on I refused a gentleman a dance."

"Ah. Pity. Well, no matter, we shall go and observe the dancing, and decide together who has the neatest footwork." He escorted her along to the ballroom and inquired conversationally, "Who was it you refused, Davinia? Some chicken-hammed looby?"

"Not at all. It was the Duke of Strathavon."

Lord Randal's shout of laughter could be heard way above the furious bowing of the violinists. "You turned up your pretty little nose at the Duke himself? And in public, with everyone watching? Oh, how astounding! How priceless! Wait until the blades at White's get to hear about this!"

"I . . . I did not think it of any consequence," stammered Davinia.

"But my dear Davinia, the Duke has never before in his life received such a rebuff. There are legions of stories about his indifference to ladies, but I have never heard tell of the Duke himself being scorned." Lord Randal took out a silk handkerchief and mopped the tears of mirth from his eyes.

"What then, was I supposed to do?" flared Davinia indignantly. "Fall in a grateful, simpering heap at his noble feet?"

She fervently hoped Lord Randal would soon lose interest in the matter. It was bad enough having to stand tapping her foot, longing to dance, without Lord Randal reminding her that it was the loathsome Duke who had placed her in this disagreeable situation.

Fortunately, Lord Randal was eager to show

her a new, chased silver snuffbox he had purchased that morning.

"Pure extravagance, I must confess, as I already own a score of the things," he grinned unrepentantly. "But I'm aiming to level with Mr. Brummell. He boasts he has three hundred and sixty-five snuffboxes. One for every day of the year."

Glad that the Duke was now forgotten, Davinia gladly turned her attention to a lively discussion of the eccentricities of Beau Brummell. But her reprieve was short-lived. In the carriage on the way home Lady Lydia and Charlotte could talk of nothing else but Davinia's refusal of the Duke.

Charlotte, for once, took her cousin's side. "After all, Mama, the Duke is *my* beau. It was I he singled out for the first two dances. I regard it as uncommon loyal of Davinia to avoid taking the floor with him."

"That may be, but there was no cause for you to be so abrupt in your refusal, Davinia. You could easily have pretended you had turned your ankle, or were fatigued, or had a headache."

Dear me, not *another* headache, groaned Davinia inwardly.

"For a girl with no title, and not a penny to call your own, you are impudently high in the instep at times, Davinia. It was most rude of you simply to walk away from the Duke as you did. Are you aware that he left the Ball shortly afterward?"

"No, Aunt, I did not know that," said Davinia with a touch of asperity. "Unlike most of the ladies at the Assembly Rooms I did not keep a hawklike watch over the Duke's every trifling movement."

Lady Lydia sighed. "Sometimes, Neice, you can be so irritatingly obstinate. I—"

"Davinia has a perfect right to refuse to stand

169

up with whoever she chooses," interrupted Sir William firmly. "Let us hear no more of the matter."

Restlessly, Lady Lydia turned to Charlotte. "You, at least, conducted yourself with propriety this evening. Tell me, did the Duke converse with you at all whilst you were dancing?"

"He was most amiable," admitted Charlotte, "though of course he did not smile once. But he asked me, in the most kindly fashion, about my London Season, and the balls and concerts I attended there."

Lady Lydia sat back in her seat, well satisfied. Davinia's eccentric behavior was, in fact, of no consequence. A gentleman of the Duke's rank and social standing would hardly pay attention to the awkward manners of a penniless orphan. The important thing was that all of Bath had seen him dance the first cotillion with Charlotte. By tomorrow morning the Pump Room would be buzzing with the intelligence that it was only a matter of time before Miss Sinclair's engagement to the Duke was announced.

A week later, Lord Randal came to call on the ladies at Chartcombe Court. As he entered the Green Salon he was immediately assailed by the atmosphere of discontent that lay heavy in the sultry afternoon air.

Lady Lydia lay upon the sofa, languidly fanning herself and declaring plaintively that she would soon expire in this excessive heat.

Charlotte was out of temper because, since the Summer Ball, she had heard nothing of, or from, the Duke.

Davinia, too, was not her normal, lively self. For some unaccountable reason she had lately been feeling listless and out of sorts. She attributed her lassitude to the hot August weather, consoling herself that at the first sign of a welcome, cooling breeze she would feel more cheerful again. She was glad of the diversion afforded by Lord Randal's call, and grateful for his attempts to lighten the tension in the Green Salon.

"What a delightful room this is, Lady Lydia," he commented. "So perfectly situated with the view across the lawns to the Rose Garden."

"It is the coolest room in the house when the weather is so oppressive," murmured Lady Lydia. She dabbed a cologne-soaked handkerchief to her forehead. "Charlotte, kindly draw your chair away from the window. The sun is streaming directly on to your face."

"But, Mama, I am so hot. I must get some air!"

"If you persist in sitting in the sun you will suffer from ugly freckles. Come into the shade this instant."

Sulkily, Charlotte did as she was bid.

Lord Randal said brightly, "I have some news to cheer you, Miss Sinclair. Are you aware that the Duke of Strathavon has fixed on a date for his costume ball at Avonley Chantry? It is to be held on August twenty-third."

"Oh!" cried Charlotte. "A costume ball! How exciting! This is indeed good news, Lord Randal."

Lady Lydia said frigidly, "I find it strange that you are already acquainted with details of the ball, Lord Randal, whereas we have not yet received our invitations."

"Oh, I happened to chance upon the Duke in Duffield's Library this morning, and he gave me the news then. But I am confident," Lord Randal

171

went on hastily, "that the Duke intends to call and deliver *your* invitations personally. I know he is most anxious that you should all attend."

Mollified, Lady Lydia regally inclined her head.

"A costume ball," mused Davinia. "I wonder what we should wear, Charlotte."

"I have no ideas at all," wailed Charlotte. "Mama, tell me how I should dress."

"By chance," replied Lady Lydia, "the latest issue of the *Lady's Magazine* has some drawings of the costumes worn by the *ton* at Lady Sopwith's Park Lane ball."

Davinia stood up. "I noticed the magazine in the morning room. I'll fetch it for you, Aunt."

"No, no!" exclaimed Charlotte. "I will bring it to you, Mama. Er . . . Davinia, why don't you show Lord Randal the bowling green? I am sure he will find it most interesting."

"I most certainly would," said Lord Randal, exchanging a laughing glance with Davinia. "I have long been fascinated by bowling greens. Tell me, has the greenskeeper been much plagued with moss this summer? . . ."

As they stepped outside onto the lawn, Lord Randal whispered, "I am glad to have the opportunity of a few words alone with you, Davinia. But whatever is your cousin about, urging us so hastily into the garden?"

"She feared that I would look at the *Lady's Magazine* first, and lay claim to the most original costume," smiled Davinia. "But with me out of the way for half an hour, she is free to choose a gown that will set her off to best advantage."

She took a deep breath. The summer air was heady with the scent of roses and newly cut grass.

"My, but it is hot today. Come, let us walk in the shade. See, even the bees look drowsy with the heat."

"Never mind the bees," said Lord Randal impatiently. "I called today with the express purpose of telling you that I have found the third letter of the riddle!"

"Lord Randal! This is wonderful news! Tell me quickly, what is it?"

He was not to be hurried. "It suddenly occurred to me to have another look at that portrait of Violetta and her husband, Roland. Just to insure that the date I gave you was correct."

"And was it?"

"Indeed yes. It was painted in 1770. So we can be certain that the fourth letter is most certainly *L* for the *Lower Rooms*. But whilst I was studying the portrait I realized something else."

He paused to brush some thorny twigs from the path, lest they tear Davinia's muslin dress.

"I had completely overlooked that, upon her marriage, Violetta would have ceased to be a Maunsell. She would, naturally, have taken her husband's surname."

"Which was?" breathed Davinia.

Lord Randal smiled. "York. Remember:

To my third, unlike Royalty, I never roam,
Yet it seems as familiar as my own home!

Davinia clapped her hands. "Of course! York is by tradition a city much favored by Royalty. Think of the Duke of York—"

"And in addition, it is probable that husband Roland himself hailed from the city, or nearby. Obviously, he would have told Violetta tales of his

173

childhood and so in time she would have felt that she really knew York almost as well as her own home town."

"Yes, it fits perfectly," agreed Davinia. "So that gives us *NAYLOV* – . And what was the last clue—

My last in shape is almost where I be,
And the name of the monarch who shelters me.

"What can it mean, *almost* where I be?" demanded Lord Randal. "Really, Violetta must have been a most infuriating woman. I am beginning to have some sympathy for Roland. Either the jewels are in this place, or they are not. How can they be *almost* there?"

"I don't know," said Davinia thoughtfully. "But I am sure that the last letter must be an *E*. If you think about it, there is no other vowel that would make sense."

"*NAYLOVE*," muttered Lord Randal. "That does not—wait! Why, yes, of course! Nay, love! Violetta adored her husband, but she was determined not to let him have the jewels. I have done it, Davinia! I have solved the riddle!"

"Not quite," laughed Davinia. "We still have to unravel *Naylove* into another word, which should give us the exact location of the jewels."

To find my whole toss the letters in the air,
'Tis a splendid place—but enter if you dare!

quoted Lord Randal. "Now what can Violetta mean by that?"

"Somewhere magnificent, but rather frightening too," pondered Davinia. "Could it be the crypt of a church, perhaps? That would make a fine hiding place for jewels."

174 __

"That might be it," agreed Lord Randal. He pulled out his pocket watch and exclaimed. "Dash it, I must get back to Bath. Strathavon is coming to dine tonight, and I must ensure that my steward has the claret at the right temperature. Last time it was a mite chilled and the Duke informed me that it was quite undrinkable."

As soon as the Green Salon doors closed on Lord Randal, Lady Lydia and Charlotte returned to their perusal of the *Lady's Magazine*.

"It is difficult for three of us to glance at it at the same time," declared Charlotte, shielding the periodical from Davinia's view. "You shall see it later, Cousin."

"There is plenty of time," smiled Davinia. "After all, the ball is weeks away." She stifled a yawn. "In truth, I am feeling a little fatigued with the heat. If you will excuse me, I should like to rest awhile in my chamber."

Once safely upstairs, Davinia seated herself at her writing desk and wrote, in a circle at the top of a piece of paper:

Underneath, she added the names of all the churches she could think of in Bath. There was the Abbey, of course, and Walcot Church, St. James's, and St. Mary Magdalene.

The Abbey Davinia discounted as a hiding place for Violetta's jewels. Violetta had already used it for her second clue, and would have been unlikely to draw upon it a second time. Also, the Abbey attracted visitors from all over the south of England, and it would have been difficult for Violetta to slip in unobserved and conceal the jewels.

But when Davinia considered the other churches on her list, she was finally forced to admit defeat. The names of none of them could be formed from *NAYLOVE*.

Davinia paced up and down her chamber for a while, willing inspiration to strike. I will not give up, she thought. I will not. I shall try a completely different approach.

She sat down once more and began to form as many words as possible from *NAYLOVE*. Few of the words made any recognizable sense, but that did not worry her. It was simply a question of eliminating all possibilities until she arrived at the one and only answer. And Davinia was prepared to sit there all night, if necessary, until the riddle was solved.

Accordingly, she wrote down *Leanovy* . . . *Lyoneav* . . . *Novelay* . . . *Envolay* . . . *Evaylon* . . . *Anveloy* . . . *Avenloy* . . . *Avonley* . . .

"*Avonley!*" Davinia cried aloud as the word seemed to jump off the paper and dance before her delighted eyes.

The notion that the jewels were hidden in a church had led her up a complete blind alley. But could the answer really be Avonley?

Oh, how I wish Lord Randal were here, thought Davinia frantically. He might be able to tell me if Violetta spent much time at Avonley Chantry. It seems probable, for Violetta was a Maunsell before her marriage, and the Maunsells are related to the Dukes of Strathavon. And if the family disapproved of her marriage, it also seems likely that they would have barred Roland from Avonley, especially when his gambling exploits became so notorious.

Davinia threw down her quill. It is all conjecture! I cannot be sure.

She took out the piece of parchment written in Violetta's handwriting and studied it again. The answer lies here, Davinia reflected. I am convinced of it. Somewhere in this riddle is an important point which I am not seeing clearly. If only the veil would lift!

She read each clue again very carefully. Suddenly, she threw down the parchment in triumph.

Oh, how could I be so blind! All is clear to me now! The answer is in the final clue: *My last in shape is almost where I be.* Avonley Chantry is an Elizabethan mansion. The house itself is built on the lines of a letter E, only with the middle bar missing. That is what Violetta meant by *almost*. Confusing admittedly, but then I have observed before that Violetta's rhymes are not exactly elegant. However, she was writing them under considerable pressure, so one should not expect too much.

And the name of the monarch who shelters me. That's easy, mused Davinia. I remember noticing most particularly a fine portrait of Queen Elizabeth at Avonley Chantry. In fact, I am sure I included it in one of my sketches of the house.

From the writing desk drawer she pulled out her sketch folder. Yes, there was the Royal portrait, rather poorly sited in Davinia's opinion, crowded in with a dozen or so other oil paintings in the magnificent Long Gallery at Avonley Chantry.

Dazed with her success, Davinia opened the window for a breath of air. The sun had hazed over now, but the atmosphere was still oppressive. Never-

177

theless, Davinia's earlier lassitude had fled. Now she was consumed with a burning desire to go to Avonley Chantry and unearth the jewels.

For some time she struggled with herself over the notion. Common sense counseled caution. After all, the Duke had forbidden her even to enter the Avonley Chantry grounds, let alone break into the house! Would it not be wiser, then, to wait until she saw Lord Randal, tell him what she had discovered, and let him go and regain the jewels?

No! thought Davinia defiantly. It may be days before I have the opportunity to speak to Lord Randal again. I simply cannot wait that long! I am in a fever of impatience! Besides, tonight the Duke will be away from home, dining with Lord Randal. It will be simple for me to slip into Avonley Chantry quite unobserved. And how delighted and amazed Lord Randal will be when I hand him the treasure.

Davinia's mind was made up. I shall go to Avonley Chantry directly after dinner, she decided, her heart beating with wild elation. And if all goes well, by midnight I shall be safely home, with the jewels in my possession!

Ten

Over dinner, Davinia's absorption in her own private thoughts was scarcely noticed by her cousin and aunt, who were still embroiled in the question of what to wear to the Duke of Strathavon's costume ball.

Sir William, in jocular mood, remarked, "Of course, you are aware that when Queen Anne visited Bath she was welcomed by two hundred of the local maidens, all dressed as Amazons. That would make an arresting tableau for you!"

"On the contrary, William. It sounds extremely vulgar," shuddered Lady Lydia. "I am convinced Her Majesty was not at all entertained. I cannot imagine what you find so amusing about this discussion of our costumes, William. Indeed, instead of entertaining yourself at my expense, you would do well to direct your attention toward yourself. Have you devoted a moment's thought to what *you* will wear to the ball?"

"*I?*" Sir William choked on his roast beef. "Surely I will not be expected to garb myself in fancy dress?"

"I see no reason why you should be excepted," replied Lady Lydia tartly.

"The notion is preposterous," grunted Sir William. "It is all very well for you ladies to divert yourselves by dressing up as Cleopatra or whoever, but for a man of my mature years it is ridiculous." He pushed away his plate, his appetite suddenly diminished.

"Nevertheless, you will have to think of something," said Lady Lydia, "else it will seem like a slight to the Duke."

"Why not go to the ball as Lord Nelson," suggested Davinia, emerging from her reverie about Avonley Chantry and the jewels. "After all, the Admiral was resident in Bath for a while, and he remains one of your heros, Uncle. And all you would require by means of extra dress would be an eye-patch and an impressive admiral's hat."

"That's a capital solution!" beamed Sir William, looking pleased. "Yes, I believe I could carry that off rather well. Now, Lydia—"

"If you are going to suggest that I accompany you as Lady Hamilton, then kindly think again," drawled Lady Lydia.

"What will be your costume for the ball, Davinia?" asked Charlotte, clearly bereft of any inspiration for herself.

"I shall decide nearer the time, when I have received my invitation," replied Davinia. She was aware that if she declared she was going as anything even as absurd as a mermaid, Charlotte would immediately claim the idea as her own.

"Ah yes, the invitations," murmured Lady Lydia. "No doubt the Duke will call tomorrow afternoon. Charlotte, you must tell Annie to put your hair in rags in the morning. Your curls are looking decidedly limp."

"Why is the fashion always for curly hair?" sighed Charlotte, enviously eyeing Davinia's golden ringlets. "If I have to be Duchess of Strathavon, I shall immediately set the mode for straight hair."

"You will do no such thing," scolded Lady Lydia. "And what is this talk of *if I have to be duchess?* You should consider yourself fortunate that the Duke is paying you so much attention. Which other bachelor in the county do you imagine would offer for your hand?"

Charlotte subsided into a sulky silence, but looked so miserable that after dinner Davinia cheerfully permitted her cousin to beat her at loo. Charlotte cheated shamelessly but as it improved her temper Davinia really did not mind.

Davinia then excused herself from the party in the drawing room, saying she had some letters to write. In her bedchamber, she took out all her sketches of the interior of Avonley Chantry, and committed them to memory. Then she ran softly down the back stairs, and slipped quietly from the house by the garden door.

The light was fading fast this evening, as the sky had clouded over and there would be no moonlight to guide her. No matter, thought Davinia. I know every inch of the way. From over the hills came the boom of thunder, and Davinia guessed that the residents of Bath must at this moment be suffering from a considerable downpour.

She was relieved to find the old iron gate still not locked. "No doubt," she murmured to herself, "the Duke has more important matters on his mind. Though with his obsessive urge for privacy I am surprised he has not ordered a moat to be dug around Avonley Chantry."

Instead of taking her usual path through the apple orchard, Davinia turned right, through the kitchen garden which led up to the servants' wing of the great Elizabethan manor house. A few months ago, the garden had been in chaos, choked with weeds and overrun by chickens and goats. But now the earth was freshly dug, and the growing beds raked to a fine tilth, ready for the planting of seeds for next year's produce.

Gardners had been hard at work, too, on the main gardens of Avonley Chantry. The tangle of wild undergrowth and long grass had been cleared away and the area around the house gently landscaped. Aware that all the work had been executed under the Duke's personal supervision, Davinia was forced to admit that he possessed excellent taste and judgment.

There was nothing about the gardens which offended the eye. No monstrous statues cluttering up the lawns. No crumbling follies. No artificial waterfalls. Instead, the newly cut lawns, the well-positioned flowering shrubs and bushes were a delight to see. By next summer, the view from the house will be one of the finest in southern England, realized Davinia, with a wistful feeling of sadness that she could not be here to enjoy it.

Davinia cautiously entered the house by a small door to the side of the Gun Room. From the servants' quarters came the sound of laughter, mingled with the clanking of tankards. No doubt, smiled Davinia, the Duke's staff are taking advantage of their master's absence to make merry.

She slipped into the Gun Room and lit a candle to guide her through the dark, deserted center portion of the house. Surefooted, with the memory of her own sketches to aid her, Davinia ascended the beautifully carved main staircase, which led up to the Long Gallery of Avonley Chantry.

This Davinia remembered as a gloomy, cob-webbed place. Its chipped and peeling walls had been crowded with begrimed portraits, and many of the windows had been boarded up.

Now she found to her delight that the Long Gallery had been magnificently restored. The windows were in the process of being repaned and leaded, to admit the maximum light. Only half had so far been completed, leaving the casements at the far end of the Gallery open to the darkening night sky.

The oak-paneled walls lent a feeling of warmth, and antiquity, whilst on either side of the enormous fireplace hung two gloriously rich tapestries. The fire was still alight.

This perplexed Davinia for a moment. Why should the Duke order the fire to be laid, on what had been one of the hottest days of the summer? Then she recalled Lord Randal mentioning that all the fires at Avonley Chantry had been lit, in order to help dry out the fresh plasterwork.

Near the fireplace stood a chair, and a small table containing the *London Gazette* and a half-empty glass of wine. Davinia imagined the Duke sitting there, taking his ease for half an hour before setting forth to dine with Lord Randal.

The thought of Lord Randal spurred Davinia into action. No point in standing dreaming near the embers of the fire. She was here to find the jewels!

According to my sketch, she mused, the portrait of Queen Elizabeth is somewhere at the south end of the Gallery, between the fireplace and that forbidding portrait of the old Duke.

Holding her candle aloft, Davinia walked the length of the Gallery. She found the portrait of the old Duke easily enough . . . but where was the Queen? Slowly, Davinia retraced her steps, studying every inch of the paneled wall, and each portrait and watercolor. Soon she found herself back at the fireplace. There was definitely no portrait of Queen Elizabeth.

It *must* be there, thought Davinia in despair. I recall it so distinctly. I devoted half an hour to my sketch of it. But . . . oh, now I know what must have occurred! With sinking heart Davinia remembered the Duke remarking that he was having many of his paintings cleaned, and rehung in order to display them to their best advantage.

He must have placed Queen Elizabeth somewhere more favorable, Davinia realized. And quite right too, for the poor Queen was crammed in with far too many other portraits. But how infuriating, how inconsiderate of the Duke to have chosen just this time to move the Queen!

Davinia stared blankly into the glowing embers. I am not giving up, she resolved. Behind Queen Elizabeth's portrait, there must have been some sort of secret panel. What I must do, then, is to run my hands along every inch of that wall until I find it!

She set the candle down on a low table, and set to work, gliding her fingers along the smooth
184

paneling. It was slow work. But Davinia forced herself to be patient, and to curb her natural agitation that she should be so near to the jewels—and yet so far.

Once, she was convinced she had found something. Yet when she held up the candle she saw it was only a small knot in the oak paneling. Wearily, she carried on though her arms were aching with the strain of reaching up for so long.

Oblivious to everything but her task, Davinia did not hear the first drops of rain pattering against the windows, or smell the gusts of smoke wafting from the fireplace as the wind began to howl outside.

Suddenly, her fingers froze on the wood. She had reached an old portion of the paneling and what she could feel was, she was sure, a tiny catch.

With pounding heart she fetched her candle. Gently, she pressed the almost invisible catch which had been cunningly sunk into a raised panel of the oak. To her amazement, delight and triumph, the panel slid smoothly to one side, revealing a small secret recess.

Davinia was trembling with excitement. Oh, Lord Randal, she thought, how I wish you were here now to share this moment with me. She stretched her hand into the recess. How terrible if there is nothing here at all! If it has all been a wild-goose chase . . . an elaborate joke of Violetta's!

But there was something there. A large, weighty leather bag. Davinia required two hands to lift it out and settle it on a small side table.

Almost dizzy with anticipation, she undid the leather tie. The inside of the bag was lined with velvet. And it was full, almost to the brim, with the most fabulous collection of jewels Davinia had ever seen! Brilliant diamonds, flashing sapphires, lustrous emeralds, flaming rubies, in necklaces, bracelets, clips and rings.

"Oh!" breathed Davinia, her eyes sparkling as bright as the gems. "How lovely they are! Why, there is a fortune here!"

As she spoke, the storm broke with violent fury over Avonley Chantry. Doors rattled. Timbers creaked. Wind-lashed rain pounded unmercifully on the roof and drove into the Long Gallery through the unglassed windows. And to her horror, as the wind howled outside, Davinia watched her precious candle flicker and blow out.

I'll relight it from the embers of the fire, she decided. Then I must take the jewels and hurry home. Oh, why did I tarry so long? It has turned into the most dreadful night, and I shall be soaked.

She reached out for the candle. But before her fingers could enclose it, she felt other hands, large, strong masculine hands, seizing her by the shoulders in the darkness.

Davinia stifled a scream. Terrified though she was, her courage had not deserted her.

"Who are you?" she demanded, willing her voice to remain steady as she confronted her unknown assailant. But who could he be? One of the servants, perhaps? "Let me go this instant! How dare you creep up on me in that underhand manner. The Duke will be most displeased when he learns about this! And I can assure you, his wrath is something to be avoided at all costs!"

She heard a deep, mocking laugh. The hands dropped from her shoulders. A tinderbox flared, and by the light of the relit candle she found she was looking into the amused face of the Duke of Strath-avon himself.

"Good evening, Miss Davinia," he said sardonically.

"What . . . what are you doing here?" stammered Davinia in dismay. "I imagined you to be dining with Lord Randal Maunsell."

"So I gather." The Duke's tone was dry. "Evidently you plotted to take advantage of my absence to break into my house and burgle me!"

The Long Gallery was suddenly flooded with light as footmen carrying lamps and boards hurried in to seal the open windows from the gale.

Davinia stood disheveled and stormily beautiful in the soft lamplight. "I am stealing nothing from you!" she flared. "These jewels are the rightful property of Lord Randal. I merely came to retrieve them for him."

"Oh, how very kind!" exclaimed the Duke, his words laced with acid. "And would you be so good as to explain, if it is not too much trouble, how you knew exactly where to find *Lord Randal's* jewels?"

He loomed before her, arms akimbo, a large, commanding figure of a man. Davinia had no choice but to tell him the whole story of Violetta and the riddle clues she had set her errant husband.

"Most ingenious," commented the Duke. "I congratulate you on your intelligence in unraveling the clues. But then you were ever a lady of such rare accomplishments, Miss Davinia. You run like the wind, climb trees as nimbly as a kitten, your sketches are wickedly accurate, your dancing divine. And I confess I was quite overwhelmed by—" He broke off, as if tempted to say more, but abruptly deciding against it.

He is goading me again, thought Davinia angrily. Oh, how I hate him!

"I apologize for entering the house in your absence, my lord," she declared with dignity. "I shall take my leave immediately." She stretched out a hand for the leather bag containing the jewels. But, swiftly, the Duke seized hold of her wrist.

"One moment. Despite your pretty, and most convincing tale about the jewels, it is still a fact that as they are on my property, then they are, by right, mine."

"Yours!" cried Davinia indignantly. "Why, it is because of you that Lord Randal is placed in such an embarrassing financial position! If you had not encouraged him to gamble, and caused him to sink into such debt to you, then he would not need these gems. It is all your fault! If you had any spark of humanity and decency you would willingly hand over the jewels and be glad that they have spared your cousin—your own kith and kin—from certain financial ruin!"

The Duke's reaction to this tirade was to throw back his head and laugh. "My, what a wildcat you are, Davinia! That was quite magnificent!"

"At least I have made you laugh," commented Davinia icily. "Most of Bath society is convinced that laughter is something of which you are physically incapable."

His mouth tightened. "So. You persist in regarding me as the villain of the piece. Well, so be it. But does it never occur to you to berate *Lord Randal* for his insistence in playing the tables for stakes which are far beyond him?"

"Naturally, I do not approve of gambling—" began Davinia.

"There is nothing wrong with gambling as such," the Duke informed her. "Though I must confess that of late it has lost much of its allure for me. Increasingly, I find this country life suits me more and more. However, the important point about gambling is that it is just like shooting, or fishing, or riding, or making love. The essential thing is to *do it well.* Which is a maxim you might care to emphasize to Lord Randal when next he attempts to embrace you in a public place."

Davinia flushed. "How dare you speak of Lord Randal in that sarcastic tone!"

His fingers were suddenly round her chin, forcing her to look directly into the unfathomable depths of his blazing blue eyes. "So," he said, his voice dangerously soft. "You really are besotted by my young Cousin Randal!"

"Besotted is hardly the word," retorted Davinia, determined not to wilt under the Duke's fiery gaze, "We . . . we love each other."

Once more Davinia saw that dreadful expression of scorn and contempt flicker across the Duke's face. But there was something else there, too. Something she could not define.

He dropped his hands. "Take your jewels and go," he ordered curtly, turning his back on her. "I would remind you that you are trespassing."

"I am surprised you do not have a moat and drawbridge, and hurl boiling oil on anyone foolish enough to approach," muttered Davinia.

The Duke whirled round. Clearly he was unaccustomed to anyone answering him back in such a fashion. Davinia felt a moment of panic, wondering if she had gone too far.

"I seem to recall," he thundered, "that last

time I found you wandering on my land I threatened to put you over my knee and spank you!"

"You would not dare!"

"I am sorely tempted!"

He took a step toward her. Davinia seized the jewels and backed away. Not for one second did her eyes leave his rugged, determined face. Then to her surprise, she noticed the corners of his mouth curling with amusement.

Davinia took advantage of the moment to turn and walk, with her head held high, down the length of the Gallery. Aware of his mocking eyes boring into her back, the distance to the staircase seemed like a mile to Davinia.

The Duke allowed her to reach the top step of the staircase before remarking, "Are you not aware that there is a storm raging outside? You will be soaked to the skin."

"Pray do not concern yourself with me. I shall run all the way," said Davinia with *hauteur*.

Despite the rain, her one desire was to remove herself as speedily as possible from Avonley Chantry, and the presence of its odious owner.

"You will not be able to run a step carrying that heavy bag of jewels," he quite sensibly pointed out. "I shall order my carriage for you."

"Oh no! My aunt and uncle will be sure to hear it in the drive, and then the servants will come rushing out. Please, no one must know I have been here!"

How could she possibly explain to Charlotte that she had been secretly visiting her cousin's beau? Charlotte would never forgive her. Besides, there was no question of Davinia being able to reveal anything about the jewels, and her attachment to

190

Lord Randal, until Charlotte was safely installed as the mistress of Avonley Chantry. No, it was vital that no one at Chartcombe Court be aware of her eventful visit to the Duke's residence.

The Duke sighed. "What an impossibly stubborn young lady you are, Davinia! You refuse my carriage, and I refuse to allow you to go home on foot."

"Which just goes to prove that you are just as impossibly stubborn as I," retorted Davinia.

"Then the civilized answer is to compromise. I shall escort you safely home myself."

As he spoke, the Duke's hand was on the bell, summoning a footman. Orders were issued, instructions given. Within five minutes Davinia found herself wrapped from head to foot in one of the Duke's thick cloaks, seated behind him on his magnificent black stallion.

"It won't be the most comfortable ride," he called as they set off into the windy night, "but it is better than you wandering about on your own with a fortune in jewels in your possession."

The storm had abated a little now, though the rain was still falling heavily. Lightning danced over the nearby hills, illuminating the countryside with sudden, ghostly flashes of brilliance. Davinia clung to the Duke as he guided the big horse through the dripping trees, and then along the deserted village road which would bring them to a quiet side entrance to Chartcombe Court.

What an adventure this has turned out to be, mused Davinia, still not quite able to believe that the Duke was taking so much trouble to see her safely home. Or perhaps, she reflected wryly, he is simply ensuring that I really am off his land, and not lurking up an apple tree ready to break into

Avonley Chantry at midnight and make off with the silver!

Soon the welcoming lamps of Chartcombe Court were in sight. They stopped under the sheltering branches of an elm tree not far from the garden door.

As the Duke's strong arms swung her down from the stallion, Davinia was suddenly acutely conscious of his masculine power, his physical strength. With a single arm he could, if he wished, crush the breath from her. She would be powerless to resist. And yet, when lifting her down from the horse, he had held her as if she were the most precious thing on earth to him.

She slipped off the enveloping cloak, and threw it across the stallion's back. "It is only a short step from here to the house. I ... thank you for escorting me home ... "

Davinia felt most ill at ease. Accustomed only to sparring with the Duke, this new situation whereby he was showing her kindness and consideration totally nonplussed her.

Gravely he handed her the bag of jewels. "I hope they bring you joy, Davinia."

She hesitated, strangely reluctant to leave him. She gazed up into his rugged face, searching for the right words to express her gratitude at his unexpected tenderness.

"Go, damn you!" he whispered suddenly, his voice hoarse with an emotion she did not understand. "Get out of my sight!"

Bewildered, Davinia turned and ran into the house. When the garden door was safely shut behind her, she leaned against it, her breath coming in shuddering gasps and scalding tears streaming down her cheeks.

"Fatigue," Davinia told herself when she awoke the following morning. The warm, reassuring sun was shafting in through the window. "Fatigue was what ailed you last night. After all, you had little appetite at dinner. Then there was all the drama and excitement at Avonley Chantry . . . finding the jewels, the surprise encounter with the Duke and that unexpected ride home through the storm. You cried simply because you were exhausted from hunger, and the stirring events of those fateful few hours."

After ensuring that the jewels were safely hidden under a loose board on her bedchamber window seat, Davinia descended to the breakfast parlor, intending to eat a hearty meal. She found Lady Lydia still preoccupied with arrangements for the Duke's visit, which she hoped would take place that afternoon.

The ham turned to sawdust in Davinia's mouth. The Duke! I cannot face him, she thought, panic-stricken. Not today. Not so soon after last night. He is bound to make some mocking remark that only I will understand, and I shall feel embarrassed and confused.

Why the Duke suddenly possessed this unnerving power over her, Davinia could not fathom. All she knew for certain was that at all costs she must avoid his presence for as long as possible.

Accordingly, she offered to undertake an inventory of the China Room for her aunt.

Lady Lydia was delighted. The China Room had been in disarray since the Battle of Trafalgar, last October. Sir William had decreed that the family would go into mourning for one month, out of respect for the slain Lord Nelson.

Charlotte, furious at having to wear unbecoming black, and deprived too of an outing to Lady Selina's ball, had run amok in the China Room. Fortunately, Annie had managed to restrain her before too much of the Dresden lay smashed on the floor. But there was no doubt in Lady Lydia's mind that the task of making an inventory of the remaining china was long overdue.

"If you wish to begin the inventory today, I will make your excuses to the Duke," she told Davinia.

"No doubt he will hardly notice your absence," Charlotte informed her cousin, "as it will be me he will really be coming to see."

"He will not be at all impressed if he sets eyes on your hair in that sorry condition," Lady Lydia told her daughter. "Run away at once and get Annie to curl it."

Hidden away in the China Room, carefully drawing up her lists of Dresden, Wedgwood and Sèvres, Davinia was able to remain quite untroubled by the Duke's visit. When she emerged, shortly before dinner, the thick, engraved invitation cards placed below the oval mirror on the dining room mantel were the only evidence of his presence in the house that afternoon at all.

"He did not inquire after you," Charlotte informed her smugly.

"There is absolutely no reason why he should," Davinia replied coolly. Yet she was annoyed with herself, nevertheless, for the stab of disappointment that he had not seen fit to make a single expression of regret on her absence.

However, she soon put all thoughts of the Duke from her mind in her growing excitement at the prospect of handing the jewels to Lord Randal. How surprised he will be, she reflected, smiling in anticipation of his joyful amazement.

As the following morning was fine, Davinia and Charlotte rode into Bath. Charlotte was to join Lady Selina and her daughter in the Pump Room, whilst Davinia went for her riding lesson.

But instead of making her way to the stables, Davinia called at Lord Randal's house in Great Pulteney Street. His steward informed her that Lord Randal was out, but expected back shortly.

"In that case, would you kindly inform him that Miss Davinia Sinclair called, and say that she is riding out this morning toward Combe Down."

One day, Davinia reflected, Sir William is going to discover that instead of taking riding lessons, I have been spending the time with Lord Randal. Then no doubt I shall have some awkward questions to answer!

But it was too glorious a morning for Davinia to dwell on any forthcoming difficult interviews with her uncle. Last night's storm had cleared the atmosphere and rinsed the sky to a bright azure blue. The grass on Combe Down was springy underfoot, and Davinia threw back her head, reveling in the light summer breeze and the prospect of a most delightful hour in the company of Lord Randal—the man she loved.

It was not long before she heard the gallop of hooves behind her. Turning, she watched the smiling Lord Randal approach. He was dressed in a dashing claret-colored riding coat, with his boyishly handsome face alight with pleasure as he regarded her.

Davinia reined in her horse, and asked him to assist her to dismount.

"But I thought we were going for a ride together," he said in surprise, swinging her to the ground.

"I have something to show you," smiled Davinia. "Now close your eyes. And no peeping!"

Laughing, he did as she bid.

Davinia reached into her saddlebag and was busy for a few moments. "Very well, you may look now," she declared at last.

Lord Randal's face was a wonder to behold as he gazed at the fortune in jewels which Davinia had spread on the grass. They glittered and glistened in the sun, almost blinding in their brilliance.

"Davinia! I cannot believe it! It is like a dream! *Is* it a dream?"

Laughing, Davinia held up a diamond necklace. "Here, touch it for yourself. I promise you they are all quite real."

And she told him how she had solved the final part of the riddle, and made her way to Avonley Chantry to find the jewels. "But the worst of it was, Lord Randal, that the Duke returned and discovered me red-handed."

Lord Randal groaned. "Pray, do not remind me. The evening was an unqualified disaster. The rain fell so heavily during the deuced storm that my kitchens were flooded, sending my cook into hysterics. She was quite incapable of finishing the dinner. I was on the point of suggesting that the Duke and I dine at an inn instead, when he remembered the unglassed windows at Avonley Chantry. He was afraid the servants would not remember to shield the windows from the rain, so he insisted on riding back to supervise the business himself."

"And thus he found me, in his Long Gallery with a bag of jewels in my guilty possession," said Davinia ruefully.

Lord Randal took her hand. "Was he an ogre toward you? Did he treat you badly? Because, if so, Davinia, I promise you he'll have me to answer to!"

"No, no!" Davinia assured him hastily. "Once he had recovered from his initial shock at finding me there he was surprisingly reasonable." Davinia decided not to mention her ride home with the Duke through the storm. There had been something strangely enchanting about that episode which Davinia was not prepared to share with anyone else in the world.

Lord Randal was gazing into her eyes. "Davinia, do you know what these jewels mean to us? At last I can speak freely to you, unburdened by the shackles of my financial troubles!"

He bent, and searched amongst the glittering jewels spread on the grass. When he stood up, he had in his hand an exquisite emerald ring, which he slipped onto Davinia's trembling finger.

"My dearest Davinia, you must know how much I adore you! Say you will marry me!"

Before she had time to reply, he swept her into his arms and kissed her.

Davinia closed her eyes in breathless anticipation. How she had longed for this moment! To abandon herself to Lord Randal's embrace, to feel his lips on hers, to unite her destiny with his . . .

And yet . . . there was something wrong. Lord Randal was aflame with passion and desire. Yet she herself felt oddly numb. She had expected to be carried away on a tide of ecstasy. But she felt nothing. Nothing at all!

Sensing the chill that was stealing over her, Lord Randal drew away, a puzzled expression in his blue eyes.

"Davinia, what is wrong? Forgive me, but I imagined you would have no objection if I kissed you."

Davinia lowered her eyes, thoroughly confused. "I did want you to," she murmured. "But . . . "

And then she knew. From somewhere deep within her spoke a cool, resolute voice that told her she did not love Lord Randal Maunsell.

For all this time I have been mistaken, thought Davinia, despairingly. I believed I loved him, in the way a woman loves a man. But my reaction to his kiss proves that my emotions are not strong enough. I am fond of him, yes. I adore his company. And if love is a word to be employed at all, then I perceive that I love him in the manner of sister and brother. But that is all.

Summoning all her courage, Davinia looked him full in the face. Taking a deep breath she said softly, yet firmly,

"Lord Randal, I am truly sorry. But I can never marry you."

And taking the emerald ring from her finger, she laid it back on the grass with the rest of the jewels.

Eleven

"What have I done? Merciful heavens, what *have* I done?"

The question pounded mercilessly round Davinia's troubled head the following morning as she walked by herself up Beechen Cliff. She had told her aunt that she was going to visit Mrs. Jarratt in the village.

Lady Lydia would surely have swooned with horror had she known that her niece was walking alone up the wild and windy path to Beechen Cliff. But after all that had passed between herself and Lord Randal, Davinia had been unable to face a morning of social gossip with Charlotte at the Pump Room. Instead she had felt a compulsion to be on her own, somewhere open and free, with the wind blowing through her golden hair. In time, she hoped, it would sweep away all the dreaded memories of yesterday.

Davinia was convinced that as long as she lived she would never quite recover from the shattering realization that she did not love Lord Randal Maunsell. And to think, she mused, that for all this time I have harbored such hopes . . . and presumed, indeed, that my fate was linked with his.

She laughed hollowly. That is what comes of placing faith in the glib words of a gypsy at the fair, she scolded herself. How foolish of you to have given credence to the woman when she told you your destiny lay with a tall, blue-eyed man whose name began with an *M*.

But I believed her because I wanted to believe, Davinia sighed. I already imagined myself half in love with Lord Randal. And the gypsy merely appeared to confirm what I desired to hear. For once Charlotte was right. Next time we attend a fair, I shall devote myself to the harmless pleasures of the hoop-la stall, and firmly turn my back on the gypsy's booth.

He had been totally stunned and disbelieving when Davinia had blurted that she was unable to marry him.

And he was quite justified in feeling so totally bewildered. I must own that it is entirely my fault, Davinia accused herself wretchedly. All through this spring and summer I have given him every encouragement in his attentions. Not once, by deed or word, have I hinted that I found his company unwelcome. Naturally, he imagined that a penniless orphan like myself would be quite overcome at his offer of marriage. The notion of refusal simply never crossed his mind.

"But, Davinia," Lord Randal had stammered, "I do not understand. Are you telling me that I have a rival for your affections? That you have another beau?"

"There is no one else in my life," Davinia had answered truthfully. "It is just . . . oh, this is unbearably difficult to explain . . . I had imagined myself in love with you. But now I know for certain that I am not. And I could never marry for anything other than love. I am so very, very sorry, Lord Randal."

The tears had rolled down her cheeks, falling like rain onto the jewels which still lay shimmering in the grass at their feet.

Lord Randal had seized her by the shoulders and cried desperately, "But we have had so much fun together, Davinia! This hunt for the jewels . . . unraveling the clues. Dash it, there is no other girl I'd rather have had by my side during such an adventure!"

And that was the crux of the matter, mused Davinia sadly. For she realized now that she regarded Lord Randal in the light of the brother she had never had. With his impish sense of humor, his teasing, his boyish grin, he had brought to the surface all her feelings of sisterly affection. Davinia cursed her stupidity for not recognizing it as such . . . for imagining her emotions to be those of true love!

Yet when Lord Randal kissed her, she had known instantly that she could never give herself to him as his wife. She had experienced no flaming desire, no tide of passion, no wild flood of ecstasy.

In truth, no man had ever kissed Davinia in such a fashion. But she knew instinctively that she would recognize the man she was destined to marry by her immediate rapturous response to the touch of his lips on hers.

Davinia raised her eyes to the blue sky and laughed. "My, just harken to Miss Davinia Sinclair! Here am I, without a penny in the world to call my own, with no great social rank or prestige, talking as if all the eligible young men in southern England are simply lining up ready to propose to me!"

"You have thrown away your best, your only chance, you foolish girl," Lady Lydia would scold reproachfully, if she knew of the proposal. Oh, what a relief that Aunt Lydia had been too preoccupied with Charlotte's marriage prospects to concern herself with Davinia's friendship with Lord Randal.

A friendship which was now, irrevocably, at an end. Finally and painfully, Davinia had managed to convince Lord Randal that they could never be wed.

"By Jove, I never imagined you would turn me down, Davinia," he declared as he mounted his horse.

"What will you do?" asked Davinia miserably.

He laughed, his eyes alight once more with optimism. "Do? Why, with a fortune in jewels in my possession, the world is my oyster!"

And with the jewels secure in his saddlebag, he had ridden back alone into Bath.

He is charming, titled and rich. He will find himself a bride before long, Davinia reasoned, as the top of Beechen Cliff came in sight.

Indeed, there are many who would consider me reckless and foolhardy in spurning him. I know of a score of girls who would not care a pin about love, and who would have been glad to marry the Earl of Belwood's heir. It is not as if Lord Randal is old or disfigured. He is in truth an extremely eligible, presentable young man.

Even if one did not love him at all, married life would still have been most tolerable with him. I should have had my own household, we would have attended every fashionable gathering, and been everywhere received. A far more agreeable existence, many would say, than that of an orphaned girl living on her uncle's charity, with not a marriage prospect in sight!

What *is* the matter with me, sighed Davinia. What perverse instinct is it that drives me to reject second best, in favor of real, true love? After all, how do I know that there really is such a love of the depth I yearn for? How much evidence of it do I observe around me in the married couples of my acquaintance?

It is difficult to imagine my aunt and uncle ever being passionately in love. The mere notion of so much emotion would be enough to have Aunt Lydia calling for her smelling bottle. And everyone is aware that Lady Selina's was an arranged marriage. Whilst Sir Richard Irwin and his lady loathe each other to such an extent that they communicate almost entirely by written notes.

Can it be, wondered Davinia, that true love is merely a device invented by lady novelists? That it really does not exist in real life? Oh, what a dreadful idea.

But then Davinia remembered her own parents. Her pretty mother, so spirited and inventive. And her adored father, ruggedly handsome with twinkling blue eyes.

There had been times when Davinia had come upon them unexpectedly. On one occasion, Davinia recalled that she was quite small, and being unable to sleep had crept downstairs from the nursery. The drawing room doors were open, revealing Davinia's mother lying on the sofa near the fire. Her head was resting against her husband's shoulder, as she looked up at him. Davinia had never forgotten the tableau, with the firelight flickering on her parents' faces as they gazed at one another, drowning in the exquisite tenderness in each other's eyes.

Yes, thought Davinia with a sad smile, how those two loved one another. It was apparent in their every word and action. It gave them a strength and unity. No matter what disaster struck, they remained steadfast, knowing they could rely absolutely on the love of the other. It was not a love which needed particularly to express itself in words. They were both just happily aware of its presence. And it could be fired anew by simply the touch of a hand, one to the other, or a private smile that spoke volumes across a crowded room.

And that is what I desire, thought Davinia. Yes, that is what I am prepared to wait for. There can be no second best for me. No compromises. No halfhearted emotion. My love for the man I marry must be all-consuming. For me it is all or nothing. And I could never, ever, endure a loveless marriage.

But what, inquired the small chilling voice of reason from within her, what is to become of you, Davinia, if you do not find this great love of yours? It must be faced; the possibility of love such as you seek is extremely remote.

Davinia strode on, her face lifted to the sun. Lady Lydia would have been urging Davinia to put up her parasol lest her complexion become marred with freckles. But Davinia enjoyed the warmth of the sun on her skin.

Where there is life there is hope, she told herself firmly. I will not be downhearted. Admittedly, if one aims high, there is always the strong chance of a heavy fall. But if the worst comes to the worst and I cannot find love, then I shall earn my living as a governess.

"What is more," she declared boldly, "I intend to be an excellent governess. I shall never cower, drab and gray-faced, in musty schoolrooms from morning to night, afraid to show my countenance to society because I am ashamed of my profession. My dresses will be pretty, and my head held high. I shall take a pride in my work. My pupils will adore me, and because of that they will be eager to learn just to please me. What a success I shall be!"

Davinia was laughing by the time she reached the top of Beechen Cliff. She took a deep breath as she gazed down on the magnificent view . . . the city of Bath spread before her with its graceful terraces, circuses and crescents . . . the beautiful valley of the River Avon, running all the way down to Bristol . . . and the combes of Widcombe and Horsecombe, with their lush fields, orchards and copses.

"It is like being on top of the world," rejoiced Davinia, her eyes shining. Up on the windy cliff, her troubles seemed less acute, whilst Chartcombe Court, and Charlotte's sulks and tantrums appeared a blissful long way away.

Davinia was about to turn and retrace her steps when she paused, her sharp ears detecting a high-pitched whining sound. She glanced around, but could see nothing. Yet there was the noise again. It was an animal, she realized, and most definitely in pain or distress.

Davinia knew she would be late for luncheon,

and Aunt Lydia would be worried about her. But it was impossible to leave Beechen Cliff without going to the aid of the mysterious animal she could hear but not see.

For a few minutes, Davinia searched in the bushes and shrubs. But she found nothing, apart from a frightened blackbird who flew off, keeping low, chittering his distinctive warning to the other birds. So where *is* that sound coming from, wondered Davinia.

On impulse, she bent down and peered over the side of the cliff. There, on a narrow ledge, some distance below, was an adorable brown puppy with a white mark over his right eye.

"But I am acquainted with you," murmured Davinia. "You belong to little Rosie, the village smith's daughter. What are you doing down there, Patch?"

Responding to the kindly note in her voice, the puppy tilted his head to one side, and wagged his tail.

"No doubt," Davinia went on with mock severity, "you were up here chasing rabbits and in your enthusiasm you toppled over the cliff?"

Patch barked.

"The problem is," Davinia informed him, "how are we to get you up again? You are far too low down for me to reach."

The puppy sat and regarded her trustingly, his soft brown eyes bright and appealing.

Then, noticing that he was wearing an old, battered leather collar, Davinia had an idea.

"Now," she instructed Patch, as she lay full length on the grass, "I hope you are an intelligent dog and will understand what I am trying to do."

She took her parasol and lowered the curved handle down toward the puppy.

"This is *not* for you to play with, Patch. Please don't start biting it!"

Patch looked puzzled for a moment, but then seemed to understand as Davinia carefully hooked the handle round his collar.

"Good. Now if I gently pull, like this, you should be able to scramble your way up the cliff. Come on now. Come on!"

The puppy's small legs worked furiously as he tried to gain a secure footing. Davinia dared not pull too hard on the parasol for fear of choking him. For one precarious moment she found she was bearing his full weight. Although he was light, the high, swirling wind unbalanced her.

Keeping a firm hold on the parasol, she flailed frantically with her spare hand for a grip on the rough grass at the top of the cliff.

"Patch, try harder! My arm is growing tired and I cannot hold on much longer!"

Davinia was desperately aware that they were making no progress. Her right arm was growing dangerously numb and weak with the strain of pulling on the parasol. And the little dog was jerking up and down with such agitation, he was in danger of pulling her over the edge.

Just as she felt the strength ebbing fatally from her, help was unexpectedly at hand. Dazed with shock, Davinia realized that the Duke of Strathavon was by her side, and in control of the situation. Taller, with longer arms and superior power, it was a simple matter for him to reach down, seize the whimpering puppy, and hoist him up to safety.

Davinia sat on the grass, shaken and relieved. Patch, recovering instantly from his ordeal, trotted across and licked her hand.

She gazed up at the Duke who was dusting down his riding breeches.

"Thank you," she murmured. "I—"

"You are an extremely foolish girl!" he stormed at her, his lean face livid. "Why did you not run for help, instead of attempting the rescue alone?"

"I was managing perfectly well!" retorted Davinia, a flush staining her cheeks.

"On the contrary, you were in grave danger of toppling over the cliff!" shouted the Duke. "Why is it that I am always encountering you in the most unladylike situations? I discover you up apple trees, attempting to burgle my house, and now on the verge of committing suicide!"

"Since you object to me so much," replied Davinia angrily, springing to her feet, "I am surprised you did not simply avert your gaze and gallop by, leaving me to my fate!"

"Since I object to you . . ." The Duke's voice trailed away. For once he seemed at a loss for words. He shook his dark head. "Oh, you are an impossible girl! I suppose now I had better see you safely home. Again! My horse will soon be quite accustomed to carrying both of us."

"Pray do not trouble yourself. I should prefer to walk," declared Davinia, with a defiant toss of the head. She untied her girdle and fastened one end round Patch's collar. "And I must return the puppy to his owner. She will be worried about him."

"As you wish," replied the Duke curtly. "Good morning, Miss Davinia."

With mixed emotions, Davinia watched him ride away. She had to admit that it was fortunate that he had happened upon her, just at that crucial moment when she lost her balance on the edge of the cliff. But why was he always so unpleasant to her. Most other people of her acquaintance insisted that they found the Duke a most civil person. Why, then, should he persist in singling her out for his arrogant, high-handed remarks?

"I confess, I do not understand him, Patch," Davinia informed the prancing puppy. "But come, we must take you back to the village. And one thing I do know for sure—Aunt Lydia is going to be most displeased with me for arriving back so late for luncheon!"

"Now remember, Charlotte," Lady Lydia advised her daughter as the Sinclair carriage bowled up the long drive to Avonley Chantry, "you must conduct yourself with the utmost grace and decorum. All Bath is fully aware that it cannot now be long before the Duke makes a formal offer for your hand. At the costume ball tonight it is vital that you exhibit the quiet assurance of one who will shortly be mistress of the house. In fact, I should not be surprised if the Duke did not take the opportunity tonight to ask you to marry him."

Charlotte's face was ashen. "Oh, Mama, do you really think so? I am so worried about my costume. Was Marie Antoinette a wise choice after all? My wig is so dreadfully hot, and I declare I shall never be able to move a step in this heavy gown."

"You look delightful," Davinia reassured her. "And the costume truly becomes you."

"I believe it to be a most suitable choice," said Lady Lydia, who was herself elegantly robed as a Grecian lady. "You look pretty, but dignified, as befits a young lady who is soon to become a duchess."

"Quite a congestion of carriages at the door,"

remarked Sir William. "Now, Davinia, is my hat at the right angle?"

"Yes, Uncle, it is perfect. But I fear your eyepatch is incorrect. Did not Lord Nelson wear it over his right eye?"

"Bless me, so he did," exclaimed Sir William, hastily adjusting the eyepatch. "How could I forget a thing like that?"

The ladies gasped with delight as they entered the great ballroom of Avonley Chantry, where the Duke was standing by the doors to receive his guests. Tastefully decorated in cream and gold, the room was ablaze with the brilliant light of ten chandeliers and filled with the happy melody of music and laughter.

Davinia cast a quick glance at the other ladies, to satisfy herself that no one else had copied her costume. It was so original, however, that no other girl was wearing anything remotely as lovely.

Davinia's problem had been, as always, that she was unable to afford a new dress. Of course, had she approached her uncle he would willingly have footed the bill for anything she desired, but Davinia's pride would not allow her to accept further charity from Sir William.

After some thought, Davinia realized that she must fashion a costume for herself, using whatever materials she could lay hands on. The dressing-up box in the old schoolroom was initially useful. Then Davinia accompanied Charlotte to her modiste and asked the woman if she could have any leftover pieces of blue or green muslin. The dressmaker was happy to oblige, having no further use for the scraps. After several days' secret toil in the privacy of her bedchamber, Davinia had emerged in the costume of a Water Nymph.

Most ingeniously, she had sewn together the scraps of muslin and drifts of silk from the schoolroom box. When she moved they floated around her in a glorious mist of differing blues and greens . . . all the colors so mysterious and beautiful in the sea on a sunny day. With her lovely aquamarine eyes, Davinia looked the most enchanting Water Nymph.

Charlotte nervously took Davinia's arm as they promenaded round the ballroom. "Do you really imagine the Duke will propose to me tonight?"

"I am sure he will be too busy attending to the comfort of his guests," Davinia reassured her. She felt sorry for Charlotte, encased in that enormous, scratchy wig as Marie Antoinette. Her own costume was delightfully cool and airy. "You are certainly quite safe for the next hour, Charlotte, as the Duke has a long line of people to receive."

Charlotte sighed with relief. "The Duke is the only person here not in costume."

"I understand that is a tradition of costume and masked balls," remarked Davinia. "The host never disguises himself. Which is a blessing, I suppose, otherwise one runs the danger of dancing with a monk, confessing that it is *the* most dreary evening imaginable, and then discovering that the monk is, in reality, one's host!"

Charlotte's eyes were still fixed on the area near the door. "I wonder who that gentleman is dressed as a French nobleman, standing near the Duke? He looks most dashing in that embroidered coat. And see, he has just murmured something to the Duke and made him laugh. The Duke, Davinia, is laughing!"

"Mmm, a rare occurrence indeed," murmured Davinia abstractedly, trying to see if she could pick out Lord Randal's face in the crowd. He must surely have been invited, she thought. But how embarrassing it will be when we meet!

For a while, Lady Lydia, Charlotte and Davinia amused themselves by strolling round the ballroom and observing the costumes of the guests.

Lady Imogen, robed as a Moon Goddess, peered out unhappily from beneath a large silver crescent pinned lopsidedly to her hair.

"How fitting," drawled Lady Lydia. "I always said the girl had a moon face."

Fortunately Lady Selina, her ample form clad as Boadicea, just failed to catch Lady Lydia's remark about her daughter. "Doesn't Imogen look enchanting," she beamed. "The silly girl wanted to come as Joan of Arc, but I told her it was most unfeminine to go clanking around in all that beastly armor."

"I fear Sir Richard Irwin will be feeling the heat by the end of the evening," commented Davinia. "He looks magnificent as Henry VIII, but personally I should be wilting under the weight of all that padding."

"Such a pity, Lady Lydia, that the Duke has no hostess to help him receive," said Lady Selina, waving her trident and nearly decapitating a passing Turkish dancer.

Smiling, Lady Lydia rested a hand lightly on Charlotte's arm. "I believe it will not be long before Avonley Chantry has a permanent mistress."

With all the guests assembled, tension mounted as everyone began to speculate whom the Duke would invite to partner him in the first dance.

"Oh, the Duke is coming this way!" warbled Lady Selina.

"And the French nobleman is accompanying him," whispered Charlotte.

"Charlotte, do not stare in that bold fashion!" hissed Lady Lydia. "It is most unladylike."

"May I present Mr. Benedict Drew," said the Duke, introducing the dashing French nobleman to all the ladies in turn.

"Are you visiting Bath, Mr. Drew?" inquired Lady Selina.

Benedict Drew smiled. "I regret that my stay must be brief, Lady Selina. I have urgent business affairs in London which claim my attention."

"Mr. Drew and I have enjoyed a long acquaintance," the Duke informed them. "We were up at Oxford together. But I hope soon to prevail upon him to pay a longer visit to Avonley Chantry."

"Ah, now you are quite well aware that I feel unsettled if I am out of London for too long," Mr. Drew replied.

Studying the merry expression in his brown eyes, his easy good manners and engaging smile, Davinia decided that she liked him. Though his chin was perhaps a little weak, and she thought it foolish of him to underate the charms of the Bath countryside she loved so much.

Benedict Drew was smiling at Charlotte. "What an enchanting Marie Antoinette you make, Miss Sinclair. I stand before you as a mere count, but I hope you will feel that two compatriots should join their forces. I should consider myself the most fortunate man at the ball if you would partner me for the first dance."

"I . . . I should be delighted," murmured Charlotte, giving him her hand.

The Duke bowed toward Charlotte's mother. "Lady Lydia, would you do me the honor?!"

"Oh!" breathed Lady Selina, when Lady Lydia was out of earshot. "Did you witness her face when

Mr. Drew took Charlotte off for the first dance! She was quite speechless with fury!"

"But what else could Charlotte do?" asked Davinia reasonably. "Had she refused Mr. Drew, my cousin could not have stood up with anyone else, not even the Duke, for the entire evening."

And how clever of the Duke, she reflected, to ease Lady Lydia's resentment by singling her out to open the dancing with him!

Davinia had no time for further observations, as she was swept onto the floor by Henry VIII, alias Sir Richard Irwin. Being a beautiful girl, and an excellent dancer, Davinia had no shortage of partners and the hours passed quickly for her in a happy whirl of music and laughter.

She did note, however, that the Duke himself danced seldom—and then he restricted his choice of partners to married ladies only. Davinia was amused. So, he wishes to keep the pot on the fire, she thought, and all the girls guessing about his intentions. Thank heavens those intentions are no concern of mine!

Toward midnight, the heat in the crowded ballroom was intense, and Davinia wandered outside for a breath of air. It was a lovely August night, with the air balmy and a full moon shining in a starry sky.

How entrancing the gardens look bathed in silvery light, she mused as she sauntered along the path which skirted the shrubbery.

"Your money or your life!" cried a low, French-accented voice in the darkness.

With pounding heart Davinia whirled round, and found herself face to face with a tall, masked highwayman.

"I have no money," said Davinia, recovering

her poise, "and if you shoot me it will make a dreadful mess on the flagstones. The Duke will be most displeased!"

The man laughed. Still in his heavily disguised voice, he remarked,

"I have been observing you. Your dress is superb. It is all the colors of the sea, and when you move it puts me in mind of the movement of the waves. Quite beautiful."

Davinia dipped him a graceful curtsy. "Thank you kindly, sir."

Strange, she thought, that she had not noticed him in the ballroom. So tall, with such presence, and dressed so distinctively—how had she failed to mark him out?

"Are you well acquainted with the Duke?" she inquired, trying to penetrate his disguise.

"Sometimes I feel I know him only too well," came the reply. "I find his company quite intolerable at times."

"Then we have something in common," laughed Davinia.

"You do not look favorably upon him?"

"I have rarely been given the opportunity," confessed Davinia. "From the start he seemed to take against me and whenever we meet he takes a perverse pleasure in being as sarcastic as possible. However, he will soon be married to my Cousin Charlotte, which will serve him right for his arrogant attitudes."

"Has he proposed to your cousin?" inquired the highwayman.

"Not yet. But if my Aunt Lydia has her way he will find himself walking up the aisle with Charlotte before the year is out."

"And you? What about your future? Have you

a handsome young buck dancing attendance on you?"

"I would rather we talked of something else," said Davinia with dignity.

"You imagine yourself in love, then," declared the masked man, his eyes glittering in the moonlight.

"I am returning to the ballroom now," said Davinia coldly, unwilling to discuss, particularly with a perfect stranger, the painful facts of her ill-fated relationship with Lord Randal. Why, she could not even bring herself to mention his name.

"You will stay exactly where you are," the man informed her harshly.

"Do not give me orders!" flared Davinia. "I wish to return to the house!"

"At this moment your desires are immaterial. You are alone in this garden with me. No one knows you are here. I doubt very much if you will be missed for some time yet."

"Who . . . who are you?" faltered Davinia, conscious now of the vulnerability of her position. She could scream for help, but her voice would never be heard above the music from the house. She could run, but the man was large and powerful, and would soon overmaster her.

"Do not be afraid," he said, taking a step toward her.

"Keep away!" Davinia cried, her voice firm though her heart was thudding wildly with fear. "My . . . my intended will be here at any moment!"

"Oh, a love tryst in the moonlight! How romantic." The man sounded amused. Suddenly, he seized her by the shoulders, and drew her roughly toward him. "Will he kiss you, my little green-eyed water nymph? Will he kiss you like this?"

216

Before Davinia could draw breath to scream, he forced her head upward and crushed his lips onto hers. Davinia struggled, but in vain. He held her immobile against him and kissed her with the savage intensity of a man who for too long has been denied the object of his desire.

And suddenly, Davinia found she was no longer fighting him. A fire raged within her, and she matched his passion, responding eagerly, longingly to the warmth of his kiss, the intimacy of his embrace. As her torrent of desire reached its height his strong hands seemed to burn her skin through the thin fabric of her bodice, and she wanted only to surrender, to give herself to him utterly, and stay close in his arms forever.

The sound of argumentative voices from the terrace broke the spell. Dazed, Davinia clung to the masked man. With all her heart she willed him to kiss her again.

It was not to be. Abruptly, he put her from him. Without another word, he turned and strode off toward the house.

Weak and shaken though she was, Davinia still had her wits about her.

"I cannot let him go!" she whispered. "To make me feel like this! So aroused, so . . . " she blushed in the darkness. "I must know who he is. Where he is from. Everything about him. He is the man for whom I have been waiting all my life. I cannot allow him now to disappeaer into the night, to be lost to me forever!"

The highwayman, she noticed, was not directing his steps toward the ballroom, but was taking a route round the side of the house.

Strange, thought Davinia, following softly in the shadows. But he did say he was well acquainted with the Duke. Presumably he is familiar with the house also. For a second it crossed her mind that the masked man with the assumed French accent might be Benedict Drew.

"We were up at Oxford together," the Duke had said. And Benedict Drew was dressed as a French count.

But, no, it could not have been he, Davinia realized. He was shorter than the highwayman, and in any event, Davinia could now see Charlotte and Mr. Drew dancing a minuet in the ballroom.

The highwayman had disappeared into the door beside the Gun Room. Stealthily, Davinia slipped in after him, praying she would not be discovered yet again by the Duke in the act of prowling round his house!

He strode confidently up the main carved staircase and into the Long Gallery, pausing in front of the fireplace. Davinia hid behind a screen, noting that as before, there was a comfortable chair and table drawn up in front of the fireplace.

The highwayman had his back to her. Hardly daring to breathe, Davinia watched as he removed his hat, his cloak and his mask, flinging them with a furious gesture down on the chair.

He turned. And Davinia found herself staring into the angry face of the Duke of Strathavon.

Twelve

Frozen to the spot, Davinia watched the grim-faced Duke stride past. When she was sure he had gone, she emerged from the screen and threw herself onto the chair near the fireplace.

"I love him!" she whispered in anguish. "I love the Duke of Strathavon!"

Right from their very first meeting he had exercised a strange power over her. No other man she had ever met had made her feel so thoroughly unsettled.

But it did not occur to me then that this was love, Davinia reflected, casting her mind back over all her encounters with the Duke. He is quite unlike other men. He possesses such authority, such an unborn air of command—which I foolishly mistook for arrogance.

And to imagine that for all this time I have

regarded him as my enemy! It was only when he took me in his arms and kissed me . . . oh, then I knew! Without a shadow of a doubt, I understood then that this is the man for whom my heart has yearned. This is the man to whom I wish to give myself utterly, body and soul. How I long to run to him now and feel his arms embracing me once more, his hand gently but firmly tilting my face up for his kiss.

But he intends to marry Charlotte!

The realization was like a shock of ice, cooling the fire in her blood. Davinia stood up, and paced the length of the Long Gallery.

The man I love is going to marry my cousin. And it is all my own doing! I schemed and plotted and did everything possible to encourage the match. Oh, what a bitter triumph it will be when I stand in Bath Abbey and watch Charlotte walking up the aisle to become his wife. It will be the most tragic day of my life. How shall I find the strength to bear it?

In despair, Davinia rested her throbbing head against the cool windowpane. Outside, the lawns were spangled with moonlight . . . the same silvery light which less than an hour ago had cast such an irrevocable spell over a man and a girl as they kissed in the garden.

But why, Davinia wondered, did the Duke disguise himself as a highwayman and deliberately follow me outside?

Davinia's cheeks flamed as she realized the answer. Suddenly, there was no doubt in her mind that the Duke had intended all along to sweep her into his arms and compel her to kiss him.

And after the first few seconds, I needed no compelling at all, thought Davinia, her blood quickening at the memory of those passionate minutes in his embrace.

Naturally, to the Duke it represented no more than a diverting episode. He was aware that the sands of time were running out on him. Soon he must propose to Charlotte, and from thenceforth assume the sober mantle of a respectable, married man.

How irresistible, then, to don the disguise of a highwayman at his own costume ball, and enact an amusing drama with the woman with whom he had sparred so often in the past few months. What delicate irony, what triumph, to have this lady, whom you have called a wildcat, melting in your arms, submitting to your embrace, matching your fire with her own.

"I cannot bear it!" Davinia's hands flew to her face. "And worse, to think I stood there in the garden and informed the highwayman in most definite terms that I did not look favorably on the Duke! That must have been the last straw, a goad which finally decided him to have me totally at his mercy. And, oh, how he succeeded!"

Was there anyone ever as unlucky in love as I, Davinia reflected ruefully. Throughout the spring and summer I imagined myself in love with Lord Randal Maunsell. All my hopes and dreams were pinned on him. And how shattering it was to discover it was not true love I felt for his lordship.

But now I am quite certain I am truly in love, and yet the man concerned is denied me, and must never know the depth of my passion for him. Never by a look or a deed must I reveal my feelings. He will, I know, be too much of a gentleman ever to mention that incident in the garden. By my demeanor I shall maintain the fiction that the episode never happened at all. I met no mysterious highwayman. And I most certainly did not find rapture in his embrace.

Davinia realized she had tarried long enough in the Long Gallery. She must compose herself, and return to the ball.

"But how can I face him?" she murmured wretchedly. "How can I remain cool, detached and indifferent, when all I long for is to feel his arms around me, and his mouth on mine once more?"

Most difficult to accept was the knowledge that for her, this was a once in a lifetime love. She knew of many girls who professed themselves in love with a score of men in a year. But Davinia had never possessed a fickle heart.

When she loved, her passion was all-consuming, and for one man only. Yet he was denied her. And she knew, with dread certainty, that he was the first and last love of her life. As long as she lived, no other man could ever take his place in her heart.

The Duke was nowhere in sight when she re-entered the ballroom. Barlow, the Duke's steward, informed her that Sir William and Lady Lydia had already left in the carriage, but that the Duke's calash was at her disposal whenever she required it.

"Thank you, Barlow. I do feel rather fatigued. Would you have the calash sent round immediately?"

She searched for Charlotte, but seeing no sign of her, assumed her cousin must have returned home earlier with her parents.

Davinia sank with a sigh of gratitude into the comforting darkness of the calash. Even greater was her relief when at last she blew out her candle, climbed into bed and drew the damask curtains all around.

She desperately wanted the release of tears, but she was so overwrought they would not come. She lay dry-eyed in the dark, thinking of the man she loved, a man to whom she must in future present a face of totally cold reserve.

"Good morning, my dear," smiled Lady Lydia as Davinia entered the breakfast parlor. "You look a trifle pale. No doubt you and Charlotte were awake half the night cozing over everything that happened at the ball?"

"No, Aunt," Davinia murmured, slipping into her customary seat, "I have not seen Charlotte this morning. I expect she would like to sleep late. She danced for hours at the ball. I do not recall ever seeing her so gay—"

"You mean Charlotte did not spend the night in your chamber, Davinia?" interrupted Lady Lydia sharply.

Davinia shook her head. "Indeed not, Aunt."

Lady Lydia rose to her feet in alarm. "But Annie reports that Charlotte's bed has not been slept in! I naturally assumed she was with you! After all, you both came home from the ball together ... "

"But we did not, Aunt," protested Davinia. "I was under the impression that Charlotte had returned with you!"

With trembling fingers, Lady Lydia pulled the bell, and a footman was dispatched to fetch Sir William as a matter of urgency.

"William, Charlotte has disappeared!" cried Lady Lydia. "She has not set foot in the house all night."

Davinia rushed forward with her aunt's smelling bottle.

"Steady now, Lydia," commanded Sir William. "Just relay the facts."

As her aunt was so incoherent, Davinia explained about the confusion over the carriages, and how each party had assumed that Charlotte was with them. "She was definitely not in the ballroom when I left, Uncle. Yet Annie declares there is no sign of her bed having been slept in."

"What can have become of her?" wailed Lady Lydia. "There are so many rogues and ruffians roaming the country. All manner of dreadful things could have befallen her."

"Calm yourself," said Sir William gruffly. "She could hardly have come to any harm at Avonley Chantry. The Duke's guests were all most respectable. And Charlotte is a sensible, level-headed girl."

"Yes, that at least is a comfort," sighed Lady Lydia. "She, at least, is not given to wild, tempestuous schemes."

Davinia lowered her eyes, aware that the barb was intended for her.

"I shall initiate immediate inquiries," announced Sir William, his face strained. "And do not fret, I am convinced Charlotte will be home by lunchtime, with a perfectly reasonable explanation for her absence."

"I will go down to the village and inquire if anyone there has seen Charlotte," or observed anyone suspicious prowling about, thought Davinia.

Leaving Lady Lydia in the care of her maid, Davinia set off toward the village. She had barely reached the end of the Chartcombe Court drive when she heard running footsteps behind her. It was Annie, red-faced and out of breath.

"Oooh, Miss, I was afraid I'd never catch up with you. And if Sir William had seen me, well, the fat would have been in the fire!"

"What has happened, Annie?" demanded Davinia. "Do you know more about Miss Sinclair's disappearance than you have admitted to Sir William?"

"No, Miss. I told him all I knew at the time. But now this has just arrived." She gave Davinia a sealed letter. "It was handed in by a messenger, at the servants' door, with instructions that it was to be given to you, most privately."

"Who was the messenger?" asked Davinia. "Did you recognize him?"

Annie shook her head. "Never seen him before, Miss." Her eyes dropped to the letter in Davinia's hand. Clearly Annie was burning to know its contents.

"Very well, Annie. Thank you. If I need you again, I will call you," smiled Davinia.

Her face registering her obvious disappointment, Annie turned and made her way back to the house.

Taking no chances, Davinia slipped away from the drive, into the shady cool of some laurels before breaking open the seal on the letter.

She half expected it to be from Lord Randal, some kind of formal indication that although their romantic association was at an end, he hoped they might remain good friends.

The letter was not from Lord Randal. To her amazement, Davinia found herself staring at Charlotte's spidery handwriting.

My dear Davinia, how surprised you will be to receive this! I am still quite overcome with shock myself at all that has happened to me in the last few hours.

I am writing to you instead of Mama and Papa, as I would be most grateful if you would go to them, and break my news gently, as I could never do in a letter. Oh, Davinia, I am so excited! I have eloped, with the most wonderful, dashing, handsome, charming man in all the world!"

Davinia rubbed her eyes, and read the last sentence again. Charlotte, who would never say boo to a goose, had *eloped?* The idea was preposterous. Yet there it was, in black and white, in Charlotte's own handwriting. But who has she eloped with, wondered Davinia. Swiftly, she read on.

I feel a quite different person when I am with Benedict. He—

Benedict Drew! The gentleman dressed as a French count at the ball. Well, whatever next, thought Davinia, feeling quite dazed as she cast her eyes down to the letter once more.

He says we are to be married at Gretna Green, and then we will make our home in London. Isn't that romantic? I am so happy. But I am terrified of what Papa will say, so you must tell him for me. Emphasize that there is no point in trying to stop the wedding, as we are traveling night and day to Scotland. Benedict is quite rich, and very respectable and I love him. The coach is here now so I must close. Thank you for helping me.

Your loving cousin, Charlotte.
PS. I never wanted to marry that horrid Duke anyway!

Stunned, Davinia read the letter through again. One thing was certain. It was the genuine expression of a girl truly in love. There was clearly no question of Charlotte's having been abducted and forced at knife-point to write these words.

Davinia was delighted that her cousin had so

unexpectedly found happiness. But she was not looking forward to breaking the news of the elopement to Sir William and Lady Lydia. Davinia could well imagine Sir William's outraged reaction:

"Benedict Drew? But who is he? Where is he from? What do we know about the fellow? Damnit, the man must be a thoroughly disreputable character, to carry my daughter off like that! Is there anyone at all in the county who will vouch for him?"

Yes, there *is* someone who is an intimate of Benedict Drew's, mused Davinia. The Duke of Strathavon! I should not be surprised if the Duke himself did not have a hand in this affair. Elopements are not, after all, arranged at a moment's notice. It would have been impossible for Mr. Drew to spirit Charlotte away from Avonley Chantry without the Duke's assistance.

Well, determined Davinia, this must be investigated before I speak to Sir William. If the Duke does know more about this affair, I shall make him come to Chartcombe Court and explain himself to my uncle!

Fired with resolve, Davinia retraced her steps up the drive, and then turned away down the side of the bowling green, toward the iron gate leading into the Avonley Chantry estate.

It was only as she closed the gate behind her, and set forth for the house that the full implications of Charlotte's elopement came home to her. There was no question now of Charlotte marrying the Duke. He was free! A tide of elation flooded through Davinia. Could it be, then, after all, that his affection for her mirrored her own for him? That kiss . . .

With a great effort of will, Davinia took a firm grip on her emotions. He has never told you he loves you, she told herself. He has always behaved most brusquely toward you. And you must not allow yourself to read too much—anything—into that kiss.

The Duke prides himself on his expertise in whatever he undertakes. Did he not tell you that? The important thing, he said, whether it be riding, fishing, shooting or making love, is to *do it well.* He is an experienced man. Of course he knows how to kiss a woman, how to ignite a fire of longing and desire within her.

But that does not mean he would wish to marry you. Particularly you, Davinia, a poor orphan! What chance have you against all the eligible heiresses who will be throwing themselves with renewed vigor at the Duke as soon as Charlotte's elopement becomes common intelligence.

By the time she reached Avonley Chantry Davinia was fully in control of herself. She found the house a bustle of activity as servants cleared up after last night's ball. Barlow informed her that his master was in the library.

"I know my way," Davinia smiled. "And do not trouble yourself, Barlow. I can see you are extremely busy. I will announce myself."

And seize the advantage by surprising the Duke, she thought.

When she entered the library, he was seated in a deep leather armchair. A book was resting on his knee, but he was not reading. In fact he seemed lost in grave thought.

The Duke leaped to his feet as Davinia swept in.

"Good morning, my lord. I should be grateful if you would give me an explanation for the contents of this letter," said Davinia, her tone harsher than she had intended. But if she had not deliber-
228

ately hardened her voice, she knew she would have lost her hard-won control, and flung herself into his arms. As it was, she found it ridiculously difficult to meet his eyes.

He, too, seemed ill at ease. She had expected him to berate her for invading the peace of his library. Instead, he quite calmly took the letter and walked slowly up and down by the window whilst he read it.

"Well," he said at last, a small smile playing round his lips. "Your cousin sounds quite ecstatic, does she not?"

"Her father will be less than ecstatic, my lord. I anticipate that he will go up in a cloud of blue smoke when he hears the news," retorted Davinia. "Were you aware that this elopement was planned?"

"I must confess I was," he said. "But it is not, in truth, as unexpected as it might appear. You see, your cousin and Benedict Drew are no strangers to one another."

"Nonsense," protested Davinia. "Charlotte only made his acquaintance last night. You introduced them. And Charlotte certainly made no indication to me that she had met Mr. Drew before. In fact I distinctly remember her asking me who he was, quite early on at the ball."

The Duke nodded. "I gather, from a brief conversation I had with her later, that Miss Sinclair did not immediately recognize Benedict in his dress as a French count. You were unaware, then, that they had met last year, at Lyme Regis?"

Davinia's eyebrows rose in surprise. "Yes," she said slowly, "Charlotte always seemed to have very fond memories of Lyme. But she never mentioned Mr. Drew."

"I understand that Miss Sinclair was staying with

her aunt in Lyme," said the Duke. "She met Benedict and their friendship was blossoming, when Lady Lydia arrived and decided that the sea air was far too bracing for such a delicate flower as Miss Sinclair. Accordingly, your cousin was swept away to the milder climes of Bath, leaving poor Benedict to wonder if she had ever cared for him at all."

"But my aunt knew nothing about him?" queried Davinia.

"Oh no. Miss Sinclair was evidently given no opportunity to mention him. Being totally under her mother's domination she allowed herself to be removed from Lyme . . . "

"And she, too, was left to ponder on what would have developed between herself and Benedict had there been more time. Poor Charlotte," murmured Davinia.

"When they met again last night," went on the Duke, "Benedict was determined not to let her slip through his fingers again. He declared his love for her, and on discovering that it was reciprocated, he immediately suggested that they elope."

"But why?" cried Davinia. "Why did Charlotte not follow the normal procedure, and tell her parents that she was in love with Mr. Drew?"

The Duke coughed. "Because I understand that Lady Lydia had it strongly in mind that her daughter should marry . . . someone else."

A blush stained Davinia's cheeks. She turned away. "Oh yes. Indeed." How embarrassing this was! She spread her hands in a bewildered gesture. "Yet . . . I still cannot believe that Charlotte of all people would agree to run away, on the spur of the moment! She always appeared to be so lacking in confidence."

"I believe you have gained a misleading impression of your cousin's character," declared the Duke. "It is her mother who has cosseted her and given her those falsely fragile airs. When she is away from Lady Lydia's influence, I understand that Miss Sinclair is a much more spirited girl."

"Yes," mused Davinia, "she did tell me how bored she was with Bath, and how she longed to live in London."

"Then, now she will have her wish," said the Duke.

"Can Mr. Drew support her?" asked Davinia. "We know so little about him. Sir William will desire to have his family and background thoroughly investigated."

"Benedict is quite respectable, I assure you," smiled the Duke. "He has a sizable income, and houses in London and Hertfordshire. Miss Sinclair will be very well provided for. And she will enjoy the kind of fashionable social whirl for which she has longed."

"Really, you appear to know far more about my cousin than I do!" exclaimed Davinia, feeling rather nonplussed at the Duke's perception. She took Charlotte's letter from the side table where the Duke had laid it. "All is satisfactorily explained, then. I beg your pardon for disturbing you. But you will understand that it was essential for me to have the matter clear before I informed my uncle of his daughter's elopement. I will bid you good morning—"

"Wait!" The Duke took two paces toward her. "That is . . . please . . . I have something to say to you."

Surprised, Davinia paused. Never had she seen the Duke look so agitated.

He said abruptly, "I wish to apologize, Davinia, for . . . for what occurred between us in the garden last night. You are probably not aware, but I . . . I took it upon myself to disguise myself as a highwayman. I quite deliberately followed and waylaid you. What happened . . . my actions were quite inexcusable. Please accept my deepest apologies. I am most ashamed, specially as I am quite well aware that you are shortly to become engaged to my cousin, Lord Randal."

Davinia was shaking from top to toe. She took a deep breath, and said unsteadily, "My lord, I think you should know that I am not going to marry Lord Randal."

He stared at her in amazement. "But you told me yourself you were in love with him!"

"I was wrong," she said quietly. "I was gravely mistaken."

He smashed his fist against his thigh. "That explains it, then. I heard this morning that Lord Randal had suddenly quit Bath and departed for London. You refused him?"

"I did."

"Then . . . "

Blue eyes met green, in a look which told them all they desired to know. Not for all the world could Davinia have broken the spell and glanced away.

"Davinia!" The tenderness in his voice sent her flying to him. He swept her into his arms, his mouth finding hers with warmth and joyous longing.

"Oh God," he murmured, "I cannot tell you what sweet delight it is to hold you close at last. I have loved you for such a long time, my adorable green-eyed girl!"

The exquisite eyes widened. "Love me! But you have always been horrible to me!"

He laughed softly. "Will you believe me when

I tell you that I fell headlong in love with you that first day we met. When you ran away from me in the apple orchard. You looked so beautiful with your golden curls tossed in the wind, your face flushed, and your beautiful eyes so magnificently stormy. I had never met anyone like you."

"I beg your pardon," said Davinia indignantly, safe within the circle of his arms, "but I do not recall you murmuring tender words of love to me. In fact you threatened to put me over your knee and spank me!"

"Because you infuriated me, you maddening girl!" he cried. "I had never been in love before in my life! I did not understand what was happening to me. That a slip of a girl like you could play havoc with my heart seemed absurd."

"But you never gave me any indication . . . never a hint of your feelings," stammered Davinia.

"I believed your affections to lie with Lord Randal," he said. "I was furious. Convinced you were throwing yourself away on him. I was too foolishly proud, then, to show my love for you. And in truth, I felt sorry for my cousin. He was heavily in debt to me. Though of course when he comes to pay me what he owes I have no intention of taking the money. I only let him run up those debts to teach him a lesson, in the hope that he would consider his fingers sufficiently burnt for him to avoid gambling hereafter. But I felt that in all decency, I could not make a play for the woman he loved. At least, he thought he loved you?"

"Lord Randal is not yet ready for marriage," smiled Davinia. "You were right about that. As you seem to be about most things. A few years will lend him maturity, and then he will find someone else and be happy with her." She went on softly, "And you really never harbored any feelings of affection for Charlotte?"

He stroked her hair. "Never. I wanted only to marry you!"

"Yet at the Summer Ball," Davinia protested, "you set everyone's tongues wagging by asking Charlotte to partner you for the first two dances!"

The Duke laughed. "Only because I was practically bludgeoned into it by Lady Lydia! She cornered me, and informed me that dear Charlotte danced the cotillion quite divinely. So what was a gallant gentleman to do?" He held Davinia close. "Do you recall that ride back to Chartcombe Court after the storm? Such a fever of love I felt for you that night. Yet I could not say a word for you, as I thought you were attached to Lord Randal. The following day I came specially to the house on the pretext of delivering invitations to my ball. But in reality I hoped to see you."

"I was hiding in the China Room," confessed Davinia. "I knew by then that you affected me powerfully, but I did not understand why." She sighed. "But you must confess, my lord, that from your attitude I could in no way suspect that you were in love with me. I declare, you played not merely me, but all Bath society false, by allowing us to imagine that Charlotte was the object of your affections."

"*I* have played you false?" queried the Duke with mock severity. "No, it is you who are the mistress of double dealings, *Madame Dresson!*"

Davinia's lovely face was a picture of guilt. "Oh, you knew!" She beat her fists against his chest. "You knew all the time. You sat before me straight-faced and allowed me to imagine I was deceiving you!"

Laughing, he seized her hands in his. "No, I confess that at the supper party you duped me completely, you clever little minx. But I took the precaution of consulting another Tarot card reader. And it soon became apparent that Madame Dresson was no more than an elegant fake. You made several small, but significant mistakes, Davinia, mainly affecting the cards which were reversed during your interpretation. As your entire reading was most ingeniously devised to urge me up the aisle with your cousin, I naturally concluded that Madame Dresson was in reality a member of the Sinclair family. Both Lady Lydia and Miss Sinclair were present in the salon, and neither would have had the intelligence to devise such a scheme. So I knew the culprit must be you."

"Were you angry with me?"

"No. Just infuriated, because I loved you so much."

"But you were genuinely angry with me up on Beechen Cliff when we rescued the puppy. You shouted at me!"

"Of course I did. I was out for a pleasant morning gallop, and I came across the woman I love about to hurl herself over a cliff! I was furious with you for being so reckless." His voice was low. "Love is a powerful emotion, Davinia. When in its thrall even dukes act irrationally."

Davinia exclaimed, "But how absurd! I know you only as the Duke of Strathavon. Tell me, what is your Christian name?"

"It is Malory," he smiled.

Davinia flung her arms around his neck. "Oh, how wonderful! How perfect!"

Observing his perplexed expression, she told him of the gypsy's prediction: that her destiny was

235

linked with a tall, blue-eyed gentleman whose name began with an *M*.

"Charlotte was most scornful at the notion of me consulting a gypsy. But the old woman was right after all!" exulted Davinia. She gave a start. "Charlotte! We must go at once to Chartcombe Court. Sir William should be informed of the elopement."

"And when he has recovered from the shock," laughed the Duke, "I shall make a formal request for your hand."

"Charlotte will be married by a blacksmith at Gretna Green," mused Davinia, "whilst you and I will walk down the aisle of glorious Bath Abbey. How vexed Aunt Lydia will be!"

"She will soon recover her good humor when she witnesses the contentment of her daughter and niece," smiled the Duke. "You will make the most perfect mistress of Avonley Chantry, Davinia. Do you think you can be happy here?"

"With you I would be happy anywhere," Davinia told him, her eyes shining. "But I am especially fond of Avonley Chantry. It is all so ironical," she said thoughtfully. "I devoted the summer to hunting for the jewels with Lord Randal. The trail led here, to this lovely house. Yet although I discovered the treasure, it proved quite worthless to me. Instead I found you, and love—"

"And joy for the rest of our lives," delcared the Duke, sealing his words with a kiss.

ROMANCE...ADVENTURE...DANGER...

PHILIPPA
by Katherine Talbot   *(84-664, $1.75)*

If she had to marry for money, and Philippa knew she must, then it was fortunate a member of The House of Lords was courting her. It would be difficult, though, to forget that the man she really loves would be her brother-in-law. . . . A delightful Regency Romance of a lady with her hand promised to one man and her heart lost to another!

DUCHESS IN DISGUISE
by Caroline Courtney   *(94-050, $1.75)*

The Duke of Westhampton had a wife in the country and a mistress in town. This suited the Duke, but his young wife, whom he'd wed and tucked away on his estate, was not pleased. So being as audacious as she was innocent, she undertook to win his attention by masquerading as a lady he did not know — herself!

WAGER FOR LOVE
by Caroline Courtney   *(94-051, $1.75)*

The Earl of Saltaire had a reputation as a rakehell, an abductor and ravisher of women, a dandy and demon on horseback. Then what lady of means and of irreproachable character would consider marrying him — especially if she knew the reason for the match was primarily to win a bet? When he won a wager by marrying her, he never gambled on losing his heart!

SWEET BRAVADO
by Alica Meadowes   *(89-936, $1.95)*

Aunt Sophie's will was her last attempt to reunite the two feuding branches of the Harcourt family. Either the Viscount of Ardsmore marry Nicole, the daughter of his disgraced uncle, or their aunt's inheritance would be lost to the entire family! And wed they did. But theirs was not a marriage made in heaven!

LILLIE
by David Butler   *(82-775, $2.25)*

This novel, upon which the stunning television series of the same name is based, takes Lillie Langtry's story from her girlhood, through the glamour and the triumphs, the scandals and the tragedies, the 1902 and Edward VII's accession to the throne.

ADVENTURE... DANGER... ROMANCE!

A PASSIONATE GIRL
(81-654, $2.50)
by Thomas Fleming

Passion made her a rebel, a soldier in the battle for Ireland's freedom. It sustained her in the long voyage across the seas to America. But Bess Fitzmaurice, the beautiful young Fenian, had much to learn about passion in the hearts and minds of men. . . .

A MIRROR OF SHADOWS
(92-149, $2.25)
by Dorothy Daniels

Only women descended from the Irish Queen Maeve were able to see the visions in the ancient mirror. Beautiful Maeve O'Hanlon cherished it. In its pale lustre she saw not only the face of the man she would marry, but a vision of the danger she would face as well.

PERRINE by Dorothy Daniels
(82-605, $2.25)

When the beautiful Perrine fled the gypsy camp where she was raised, she knew only that she could not bear to wed the violent man to whom she was betrothed. She did not dream that he would follow her across two continents, haunting her, sworn not to rest until he saw her in her grave!

THE MAGIC RING by Dorothy Daniels
(82-789, $2.25)

The magic ring — a lucky ring — was a gift from across the seas from the parents whom Angela had not seen since their return to Italy ten years before. Angela slipped it on her finger and made a promise to herself. She would find her parents once again, even if she had to defy the secret societies that held Italy in terror, even if she must risk her very life.

CARESS AND CONQUER
(82-949, $2.25)
by Donna Comeaux Zide

Was she a woman capable of deep love — or only high adventure? She was Cat Devlan, a violet-eyed, copper-haired beauty bent on vengeance, raging against the man who dared to take her body against her will — and then dared to demand her heart as well. By the author of the bestselling SAVAGE IN SILK.

ROMANCE...ADVENTURE...DANGER!

HOUSE OF THE DANCING DEAD
by Aola Vandergriff   *(90-018, $1.95)*
What was she doing here? Masquerading as another woman, waltzing in the arms of a pale man who claimed her with his icy eyes and cold hands. Would she still be warm, young and alive — after a year in this House of The Dancing Dead?

SISTERS OF SORROW
by Aola Vandergriff   *(89-999, $1.95)*
Between twins a fine wire is strung, transmitting the vibrations of terror and the dangers of death. When Shannon and Shelly went south to claim their joint inheritance, an old plantation called Sorrow, they discovered the family secret. Madness and murder waited here for the Sisters of Sorrow!

WYNDSPELLE
by Aola Vandergriff   *(89-703, $1.95)*
The year is 1720. A stranger steals a kiss from a beautiful servant girl, and suddenly she is accused of being a witch! She must flee — there is no time to lose. But where would she go? Only one house would accept her, that she knew with terrifying certainty: the haunted, grisly spectre of evil perched on a sheer cliff where nobody visited voluntarily—the house called WYNDSPELLE.

WYNDSPELLE'S CHILD
by Aola Vandergriff   *(89-781, $1.95)*
Megan came to Wyndspelle to care for a haunted, invalid child with no will to remember, to speak or to love. Whisperers said that the little girl had set the fire that killed her mother. Others said it was her father who had done the deed. Yet, in this desolate manor where no flowers bloom, Megan finds love blossoming in her heart for the two the world condemns — for the child and for the tormented master of WYNDSPELLE.

THE JIGSAW MAN
by Dorothea Bennett   *(89-414, $1.95)*
The man who came back was not quite the same man who had defected from British Intelligence to the Russians years ago. His only tie to the past was his daughter. Would she help him though her lover was the British agent on his trail? He was determined to live despite the efforts of two nations to capture him and his list of traitors and to close by death the case of THE JIGSAW MAN.

YOUR WARNER LIBRARY OF
REGENCY ROMANCE

AGENT OF LOVE
by Jillian Kearny   (94-003, $1.75)

THE FIVE-MINUTE MARRIAGE
by Joan Aiken   (84-682, $1.75)

DUCHESS IN DISGUISE
by Caroline Courtney   (94-050, $1.75)

SWEET BRAVADO
by Alicia Meadowes   (89-936, $1.95)

LOVE UNMASKED
by Caroline Courtney   (94-054, $1.75)

WAGER FOR LOVE
by Caroline Courtney   (94-051, $1.75)

PHILIPPA
by Katherine Talbot   (84-664, $1.75)

THE MIDNIGHT MATCH
by Zabrina Faire   (94-057, $1.75)

LADY BLUE
by Zabrina Faire   (94-056, $1.75)

WARNER BOOKS
P.O. Box 690
New York, N.Y. 10019

Please send me the books I have selected.
Enclose check or money order only, no cash
please. Plus 50¢ per order and 20¢ per copy
to cover postage and handling. N.Y. State and
California residents add applicable sales tax.

Please allow 4 weeks for delivery.

_____ Please send me your free
mail order catalog

_____ Please send me your free
Romance books catalog

Name_____

Address_____

City_____

State_____ Zip_____